LIES IN SAVANNAH

THE SOUTHERN SLEUTH BOOK 4

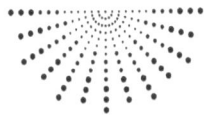

HARPER LIN

*I*t was the annual Savannah Dog Days and Firecracker Festival. Everyone from Savannah and the surrounding counties was in attendance. The sun shined brightly the first day of the festival, and already at eleven in the morning, the thermometer had passed the eighty-degree mark. Thankfully, there was plenty of shaved ice, lemonade, and root beer to be found across the acres of attractions.

Becky Mackenzie strolled the grounds with her mother Kitty and Cousin Fanny, happy to feel the sun on her face and have dozens of delectable treats within arm's reach. At the moment, she was enjoying the sticky delight that was a nest of pink cotton candy in a paper cone.

"Mama, would you like a taste?" Becky offered the cone to her mother, who she knew had no willpower when it came to sweets of this nature.

"I really shouldn't." Kitty looked longingly at the candy her daughter offered.

"Oh, Mama. It's once a year. It's not like you sit around all day eating cotton candy. You won't have another taste of this heaven until next summer." Becky smiled as she tore off a feathery chunk and handed it to her mother.

"When you put it that way…" Kitty chuckled and happily took the candy, folding the entire piece into her mouth before licking her fingers.

"Cousin Fanny, would you like some?" Becky asked. She had been making an extra effort to be kind to her cousin since they had gotten into a pinch of trouble with a gangster and his girl a while back. Of course, it had been Fanny who had gotten them into the trouble to a certain degree, and Becky hadn't forgotten that if her cousin had gone home like she'd been instructed to, the whole mess could have been avoided. But there was no reasoning with Fanny.

"Oh, no thank you. I don't like being sticky," she replied without looking at Becky. Why would she look at Becky when she was too busy smiling at every gent that passed by? That was the thing about Fanny: she was a ripe tomato. And there were plenty of farmers who wanted nothing more than to pick her from the vine.

Becky shrugged. It was too exciting a day to let Fanny ruin it with her weakly veiled jabs. The sound of the clinking metal of the rides accompanying the howls of people being swirled around on a spinning plate or lifted high in a swinging bucket was like a siren's song. There was so much Becky wanted to run off and inspect that she hardly knew where to start. Instead of dashing around from attraction to attraction, she observed every tent and booth and ride and made a list in her head of what she wanted to see when she came back later. Then the sun would be starting to set, and the cooler air would be circulating, and she'd be on the arm of her favorite fella, Adam White.

"Becky, did you hear what I said?" Kitty asked.

"I'm sorry, Mama, I was daydreaming. What?" Becky replied.

"I said, your father is expecting us to stop by the Jolly Corks tent, where he and the rest of the Elks Club will be doing their minstrel show," Kitty said. "I do hope we can find it in time to see him on the stage."

"I can't believe Uncle Judge is going to get on stage." Fanny laughed as she put her hand to her cheek.

"Your uncle can be quite the ham when he wants to be." Kitty giggled back.

"Remember my third-grade talent show?" Becky replied. "Daddy was my assistant when I did a couple of magic tricks. If it weren't for him, my silly game of hide the peanut under the cup would have been a complete disaster. He did ham it up, didn't he, Mama?"

Kitty was laughing hard, nodding as she went on to explain to Fanny how Judge had scratched his head, stroked his jaw, and screwed up his face like he was totally perplexed by his eight-year-old daughter's stunt. By the end of the yarn, all three ladies were laughing.

Just then, Becky saw a familiar figure sitting at a table inside a dark-blue tent with its flaps folded back. Over the opening in gold lettering were the words "Fortune-Teller." The woman inside smiled.

"I'll catch up with you girls," Becky said. "I'm going to say hello to someone."

"Who? Is it a young man?" Kitty asked, making Becky stare at her as if she had just sprouted a horn in the middle of her head.

"She's going to see that old Gypsy," Fanny said as she jerked her chin in the fortune-teller's direction. "Why you insist on associating with such a flimflam artist is beyond me. In Paris, if anyone mingled with the street people that way, they'd soon find themselves ostracized from all the dignified families in town."

"Oh, Becky, are you sure that's such a good idea?" Kitty worried.

"Mama, Madame Cecelia was at Martha's birthday party. If the Bourdeauxes found her and Count Ernesto worthy enough to do business in their home, surely my visiting her tent won't cause any permanent damage to the Mackenzie name," Becky replied. "I'll find you at the Jolly Corks tent."

"All right, dear," Kitty replied. "Don't be too long."

As soon as Kitty turned her back to continue walking, Becky stuck her tongue out at Fanny, who huffed and quickly kept up with her aunt.

"I see you are still entertaining your cousin," Madame Cecelia said as she motioned for Becky to take a seat on the other side of the table.

5

"She should take a long walk off a short pier. I don't think she's ever going to leave. Truthfully, I don't think anyone wants her," Becky replied as she watched Madame Cecelia shuffle a large deck of cards with silver moons on them. "I'm sorry it's been so long since I've seen you. Summer is much busier than I expected it to be."

"Does your mama have your schedule filled with perspective husbands paying you visits?" Madame Cecelia winked. Her long black lashes made her eyes look like those of an exotic cat. Since they'd met at Martha Bourdeaux's birthday party, Becky and Madame Cecelia had become fast friends. Becky never had to tell Madame Cecelia about her gift of gab with those from beyond the grave. The Gypsy recognized her talent instantly and, even more important to Becky, accepted it as if it were no different from having red hair and brown eyes.

"Thank goodness, no. She's slowly coming around to the fact that I have my sights set on a fella who isn't from the South," Becky said. "I think she's given up trying to find a husband for me."

Madame Cecelia chuckled, arched her right eyebrow, and slowly began to deal out the cards in a square pattern in front of her. "Maybe the cards will tell us something. Perhaps you'll be hearing wedding bells. Or soon, you'll be free of that pain in your *fanny.*"

Becky laughed and nodded. But it didn't take long for Madame Cecelia to become very serious. Her eyes narrowed as she studied the pictures on the tarot cards. She shook her head, looked outside the tent to the sea of people passing by, scooped them up, and reshuffled. With steady hands, she began the process all over again. But the same expression fell over her face as she realized the same cards were popping up. One in particular kept pulling her eyes to it.

"What's the matter?" Becky asked. "Let me guess. Fanny's not leaving."

"Uh, well, no. It doesn't look like she is, but..." Madame Cecelia looked up at Becky with a serious expression. "I don't think this is such a good reading. We shouldn't do it today. I am probably picking up vibes from someone else who is about to stumble into my tent. Let's do this at the apartment some time. Not here."

"Now you've got me intrigued," Becky insisted with a smile.

"I think my mother should do your reading. She's

so much better at this than me. For the locals, I can give a quick reading without much detail, and they are quite happy. Right now, I am feeling like this is totally wrong and…" Cecelia could tell by Becky's expression that she wasn't going anywhere until her fortune was read.

"What's wrong?" Becky asked.

After a deep breath, Madame Cecelia shook her head and finally began to speak. She pointed to a card showing a skeleton wearing a black cloak and carrying a scythe. It was a scary-looking card.

"Don't let the image fool you. The Death card does not indicate someone will die. If you only knew how many people run out of the store thinking they had ten minutes to live after seeing this card. It really means *change*. There is going to be a very big change in your life." She tapped the card with her red fingernail. Then she pointed to another card showing a woman on a throne with ropy vines growing all around her and an upside-down chalice over her head.

"What does that mean?" Becky asked.

"Your cup is empty," Madame Cecelia said matter-of-factly.

Becky shrugged and shook her head. If it meant

she was going to have fewer parties and gin joints to go to, that was all right. With the hot weather during the day, who had the energy to dance all night? Fall couldn't arrive soon enough.

"And in addition to that, you have the Fool, who is in conflict with the sleeping queen. I just…" Madame Cecelia shook her head. "I'm not even confident this is your reading, Becky."

"Cecelia, if I knew something was not right with you, would you want me to let the cat out of the bag? Or would you rather keep your head in the sand?" Becky leaned forward with her elbows on the table.

"The chances of you knowing before me would be so miniscule that I don't think the issue would ever pop up." Madame Cecelia tapped the cards and smirked.

"You know what I mean," Becky replied.

Madame Cecelia took a deep breath and focused on the cards. She squinted, tilted her head, and studied each image as if there might be something she was missing before she opened her mouth to speak. "I see someone close to you. I can't see the face or if it's a man or woman. Just a shadow. But this person is close to you. They've turned their back, leaving you. Someone else is waiting for them.

That's all I can see." Madame Cecelia's eyes held sadness. She didn't like giving her friend this kind of reading. But it was so clear and so strong that she knew it belonged to Becky and not someone who was just passing by.

"I don't know what you could be talking about," Becky replied. She pushed herself back from the table as if the cards might be contaminated.

"I'm sorry. I just read what they tell me," Madame Cecelia said.

"Does this person die?" Becky's heart was pounding, and her temper was rising.

"I don't know. All I know is they are leaving," Madame Cecelia replied. The cards looked up at both of them, showing off their intricate designs and worn edges while leaving their meaning no clearer than a rain puddle in the Mackenzie tobacco field.

"And have you ever been wrong?" Becky huffed.

"Of course I have. And I probably am now. Who knows what the cards are trying to tell me?" Becky knew Madame Cecelia was lying to spare her feelings. "I think it's for someone who will be visiting my tent any minute now."

Becky looked at the open flaps of the tent, but no one walked through. "What do I owe you for the reading?" she asked and opened her small coin purse.

"I don't charge my friends."

Madame Cecelia hoped after this that Becky was still her friend. Sometimes her gift was more of a curse. But she couldn't lie. She'd learned long ago that trying to say the cards said something they didn't would be even more devastating.

"I'm sure it's nothing," Becky said with a shake of her head and a weak smile. "I don't know about you, but it's as hot as a Louisiana pepper out there. I'm going to go get back to Mama and Cousin Fanny."

Madame Cecelia took Becky's hand before she left and squeezed it tight. "Come see me at the apartment. Soon."

Becky returned the squeeze and nodded before leaving with a wave. It felt a hundred degrees cooler outside the stuffy Gypsy's tent, and Becky was able to clear her head. With a few deep breaths, she felt her senses returning as she looked at all the people who were milling around, holding bags of popcorn or peanuts, laughing, and pointing at all the colorful sights and attractions. All of a sudden, a man and woman, holding hands and giggling, went into Madame Cecelia's tent. There it was. The reading that made no sense was probably for them. The seer had been right.

"Becky!" Kitty was waving madly from the entrance to the Jolly Corks tent. It was a bright-yellow and red canvas that looked as gay and inviting as if Mr. Barnum himself had set up the structure. Becky shook off Madame Cecelia's tarot card reading and hurried over to her mother.

"Is he on?" Becky asked.

"Not yet. It will be about fifteen minutes. But Mr. Rockdale is doing the most fantastic juggling you've ever seen." Kitty laughed. "I didn't even know he could juggle. Can you imagine, after all these years of living next door to the Rockdales, that this skill would have gone unnoticed?"

"Where's Fanny?" Becky asked.

"Oh, well, Fanny saw Teddy Rockdale and went to say hello." Kitty cleared her throat. It was a well-known fact to all involved that Teddy was Martha Bourdeaux's beau, and someday wedding bells would be ringing for the two of them. That never seemed to be of any concern to Fanny though. She emerged from behind a tent with a huge bouquet of pink cotton candy in one hand while holding Teddy's arm with the other.

"Doesn't like getting sticky?" Becky muttered.

"Behave yourself, Rebecca Madeline," Kitty whispered as she waved to Teddy.

"Don't I always?" Becky batted her eyes at her mother.

"The pie contest is right next door. Did you know that Gertrude Peabody is entering this year?" Kitty asked Becky. "She says she received a recipe for blueberry pie from her great Aunt Rose, who swore to never give up the recipe to anyone."

"So why did she finally give it to Gertrude?" Becky asked.

"She finally died." Kitty shrugged. "Oh, that's her boy Brian over there. It looks like he's carrying that very priceless pie. Brian Peabody, what are you doing with your mother's blueberry pie?"

"Hi, Mrs. Mackenzie." Brian was thirteen years old, tall, lanky, and awkward like every boy that age. "Mama's not feeling well. Her ankles swelled up something awful from the heat, so Aunt Genevive is over taking care of her. I said I'd deliver her pie for the contest. She made four pies before this one. Dad says he hopes he never tastes another blueberry pie as long as he lives and was glad to see this one go."

"That was mighty nice of you to help your mama that way." Becky chuckled. "You sure have grown since the last time I saw you. Looking like a regular John Gilbert, isn't he, Mama?"

"Thank you, Miss Becky." Brian blushed a dozen shades of red. "I better deliver this pie."

"The pie contest is right over there." Becky pointed around the Jolly Corks tent to a set of picnic tables with a white tent behind it. Brian gave a quick thank-you to Becky and walked quickly but carefully toward the tables.

"I can't believe how tall he's gotten," Becky said.

"Oh, he'll be a wiry one like his father. Not a hint of meat on his bones," Kitty replied.

"Teddy Rockdale, what's this I hear? Your father is an expert juggler, and you kept that a secret from all of us for how many Fourth of July parties?" Becky teased. "And here we were being subjected to your singing and piano playing."

"I thought you liked my singing and piano playing," Teddy huffed before giving Becky a peck on the cheek.

"After three champagne cocktails, I'll like a tomcat's singing and a two-year-old's piano playing," Becky teased.

"Teddy, I just love seeing you play the piano," Fanny gushed as she daintily ate her cotton candy. "I think I'd just love to…"

Just then, the most horrifying, high-pitched scream cut through the fair. It was heard over the rides and the laughter and appeared to have brought the entire fairgrounds to a halt for several terrifying seconds.

"What happened?" Teddy asked.

There was another scream. It came from the pie tent. Everyone stopped, turned, and looked.

CHAPTER TWO

*A*t first, Becky thought that something had happened to Brian Peabody. Everyone nearby took off in that direction and saw the boy standing at the entrance of the tent in front of a sign that read "Pie Tasting in Progress—Judges Only." He was holding his mother's pie but had gone slack-jawed as he stared inside the tent.

"Brian? Are you all right?" Becky asked as she got to the boy.

A half dozen other people had rushed to the scene. That was when Mr. Clem Foxworthy, wearing his Elks Club fez and a short-sleeved button-down shirt, staggered toward the door. Becky thought he was three sheets to the wind until she watched his face turn blue in front of her. His steps were wobbly and pigeon-toed, and his hands went to his throat. After that, he froze, his eyes bugged out, his tongue came out, and he whirled around before he collapsed onto the table holding all the blueberry pies, sending everything sliding into a giant purple pile of goo. Everything was tinted purple, from the fez on his head to his shirt to the white tablecloth and even the grass.

"Someone call a doctor! Is there a doctor in the house?" Becky heard from the crowd. She stood next to Brian, her hand on his arm as they both watched two other members of the Elks Club rush to Mr. Foxworthy's side. They lifted him and carried him to the picnic tables, where they laid him out.

"What happened?" Becky asked.

"I-I don't know," Brian stuttered. "I saw Mr. Foxworthy take a bite of pie, and then he-he-he just started choking."

"Brian, go on home. You don't need to stay here for this," Becky urged.

"What about my mom's pie?" he said innocently.

"I think you can tell her that the pie contest was canceled." Becky smoothed the boy's hair and gave him a gentle nudge. He held his mother's pie in both hands and quickly cut through the increasing number of gawkers.

Just as Brian disappeared, a man with a straw hat and a twitchy mustache elbowed his way through the crowd.

"Who needs a doctor?" he shouted. "Who called for a doctor?"

Becky pointed toward where Mr. Foxworthy was lying. There was no movement, not even the steady rise and fall of his chest. His brother Elks were shouting his name and tapping his cheeks with their open palms, trying to revive him, but nothing was working. Everyone pushed along behind the man in the straw hat as he pulled off his jacket and began to try and revive Mr. Foxworthy. Becky stayed back, surveying the crowd, and glanced around just in time to see a man slip out of the judges' tent.

She'd seen him before: a rummy who wandered through town only to disappear for a few weeks and return when he thought the juke joints had forgotten he didn't pay his tabs. His name was Vincent, but everyone called him No-cent, since he always spent more than he had. He didn't see Becky, and Becky was so shocked by everything happening around her that she didn't think No-cent was up to anything except trying to get a free slice of pie.

"Would everyone please back up! Back up and give us some air!" the Elks were shouting as the doctor in the straw hat did his best to revive Mr. Foxworthy.

It was no use. With sweat pouring down his forehead and his sleeves rolled up to his elbows, he stepped back from the picnic table, removed his hat, and shook his head. A collective gasp rippled through all the onlookers. Mr. Foxworthy was dead.

"Doctor, what happened to him?" one of the Elks asked. Becky carefully and quietly inched her way around the crowd, closer to the picnic tables, where the men were standing, and listened.

"If I didn't know any better, I'd say this man was poisoned," the doctor said as he wiped his brow with the back of his wrist. "See here. This would indicate that his airways closed up. His eyes, see how they are bloodshot. And his tongue is swollen to three times its normal size. Yes, I have no doubt that this man was poisoned."

Becky inched back a few paces and peeked into the tent where the pies had been arranged. They were all in a heap. The name cards of the bakers were scattered everywhere. There was no way to know which pies Foxworthy had tasted up to this point.

Just a few feet away from the excitement, standing in the shadow of a weeping willow, was

No-cent. He twisted a cap onto a small bottle before he shoved it into his pocket and started to walk away.

Without telling anyone, Becky hurried off behind him. No-cent had been loitering around the tent just as Mr. Foxworthy was doing the pie tasting. But why would this rummy, who had no family, no job, and no connection to the Elks Club, want to poison Mr. Foxworthy? It didn't make any sense.

Still, Becky followed him. It didn't take long to get away from the corner of the fair where things had come to a standstill and return to the fun and excitement. People had no idea that Mr. Foxworthy had died of poisoning just a few short yards away. They were busy trying to win a stuffed lion or ring the bell of the strong man's challenge. And No-cent wove invisibly through the crowd. Only Becky kept her eye on him and followed as he walked away from the grounds, through the tall grass, and to the line of trees that separated the fairgrounds from the Elijah Clark Forest Preserve.

Becky crouched uncomfortably as she hid among the tall blades. No-cent was leading her into the cool darkness of the woods. Her stomach twisted with the thought that No-cent had had something to do with Mr. Foxworthy's death. She watched him look around before he disappeared between the trees. Becky then turned around and saw the fair going on as if nothing had happened. Her mother and Fanny would be looking for her, and she was probably going to miss her father's performance in the Jolly Corks tent. But it would take more than her father in a minstrel show to keep her from discovering where No-cent was going.

She slipped into the trees and quickly felt the temperature drop. The air was still heavy with humidity, and the coolness clung to her skin like crepe paper to a wet post. Carefully, she looked around and spied No-cent hurrying toward a pond. She did the same, wobbling and slipping in her black Mary Janes, which were made for dancing, not combing the wild landscape.

Finally, she saw No-cent standing at the edge of the pond. He tossed something that looked like a small bottle up and down in his hands. Then, with a mighty heave, he threw it into the pond. What was it? The vial that held the poison? Becky was sure of it. But there was no way she was going to go wading through that murky water to get it.

Just as she was about to duck behind a thick, mossy tree, she lost her balance. A high-pitched squeal escaped her as she fell and landed painfully on her bottom.

No-cent looked in her direction. "Who's up there?" he growled in a gravelly voice.

Becky held her breath and listened for angry footsteps to commence coming in her direction. But she didn't hear anything. When she looked around, No-cent was gone, and she had nothing to show for her efforts but a dirty dress and shoes and a sore tailbone.

When she finally caught up to her mother and Fanny, they were furious with her.

"Where did you go? You missed your father's performance," Kitty scolded. "And what happened to your dress and shoes? Never mind. I don't want to know."

"I'm sorry, Mama. I'm sure I'll be able to catch one of his other performances. The Elks Club is putting on the Jolly Corks for the whole fair," Becky replied.

"Not now they aren't. The rest of the fair will go on. But with Mr. Foxworthy suddenly passing, they've shut down the show. Out of *respect* for one of their members." Kitty shook her head.

"Well, where is he? I'll go apologize to him myself," Becky pleaded.

She often complained about her mother's meddling and hated how Fanny was thrown up at her at almost every turn, but she loved her mother and absolutely adored her father. She felt guilty, plain and simple. No-cent had lured her away from her family, and she hadn't even gotten any solid proof he'd done anything. What had she been thinking?

"He's in the tent. But he's busy now. They all are. They've got to find Mrs. Foxworthy and tell her the bad news. Your father has taken the responsibility of breaking that awful news, because he thinks of other people first," Kitty snapped. "Fanny, if you don't mind, I'd like to get home. This entire event has given me the doldrums."

Kitty let Fanny link her arm with hers, and they headed back in the direction of the field where their automobile was parked.

Becky quickly turned to the Jolly Corks tent and went inside. It was hot inside, and a couple of men from the Elks were already stacking the chairs. She asked after her father, and they pointed to a flap in the tent that led to another tent. Her toes were stinging from hurrying along the rocky terrain. Oh, how she wanted to slap that No-cent. This was all his fault.

Is it really? her conscience whispered. She shook her head, her red finger waves bouncing along the side of her face. She didn't want to hear it. All Becky wanted to do was find her father and apologize. Finally, she saw him. She waved wildly to get his attention, a friendly grin on her face. His stern gaze nearly made her start to cry.

"Daddy! I'm so sorry I missed your show," Becky said as she looked up at Judge Mackenzie. He was rolling down his sleeves and straightening his tie.

"It's all right, Becky. Now, if you don't mind, I've got things to tend to." His voice was firm, as if he was giving orders to one of the men who worked in the tobacco fields.

"No. I mean it. I really am sorry. I got distracted and…"

"Where is your mother?" he asked as if he were mad at her too.

"She said she was feeling poorly and wanted to get back home. I just wanted to apologize first and…"

"Feeling poorly," Judge muttered and looked at the ground as if he was thinking of something. "Get home and tend to your mama."

With those words, Judge turned around and walked off to join the other Elks, all wearing their red fezzes, as they bustled about on their way to break the news to Mrs. Foxworthy. Becky was left standing there alone. She felt like the ugliest girl at a dance.

~

When Becky caught up with her mother and cousin, they were getting the car started. Thank goodness the machine needed a couple of good cranks before she'd turn over, or else Becky might have found herself walking home. She sat alone in the back seat, kicked off her shoes, and discovered huge blisters had formed on two of her toes. But that was nothing compared to the horrible silence Kitty was throwing at her.

"I found Daddy. I apologized for missing his show," Becky said and waited for her mother's approval. "He was going to Mrs. Foxworthy's home with some of the other fellows."

Still, there was nothing. Becky leaned back into the seat and looked out at the scenery going by without really seeing anything. She hadn't meant to miss her father's big moment on stage. But she had been trying to help Mr. Foxworthy. No-cent had been there, and he'd had something to do with it. Of that Becky was sure.

"I think I saw a man coming out of the pie tent after Mr. Foxworthy collapsed," she offered, hoping that might break the ice that had engulfed the whole car. "That's who I was following, and I got distracted. I think the police might…"

"When I was in Paris and a family was met with an untimely death, it was not uncommon for friends to bring over a basket of fruit," Fanny offered as if Becky hadn't said a word. Now it was getting out of hand.

"That's a lovely idea, Fanny. Why don't you do that?" Kitty said.

Becky settled into the back seat and said nothing else. It was a hot day, and her mood had been soured by the whole incident. She was sorry for Mr. Foxworthy's sudden demise, but how it had turned into such a debacle for *her* she couldn't grasp. She tried to think back to any instance in which her mother or father hadn't been able to show their support for her one way or another, but her memory failed. She couldn't drum up a single time that they hadn't been there for her. That made her feel even worse.

CHAPTER THREE

*I*t was late afternoon before Judge returned home. Becky had holed up in her room, doodling in her sketchbook. She'd drawn pictures of No-cent tossing that bottle into the pond along with a few of Mr. Foxworthy tipping over the pie tables. It was a gruesome image, but it was on her mind. Actually, Becky was trying to think of anything but her parents being so angry with her.

When she heard the car coming up the long dirt drive, she leaned out her window. Mr. Rockdale had given Judge a lift. They whispered a couple of things and shook hands. Before the car had turned around, Judge had removed his fez and entered the house.

Becky didn't know what to do. Part of her wanted to run downstairs and make sure her father gave her that same smile he always did. But she'd be absolutely devastated if he didn't. She'd need to make a grandiose gesture to get back into his favor. Literally throw herself on the mercy of the court. She squared her shoulders, took a deep breath, and tiptoed downstairs. She was surprised to find Judge and Kitty having a low but heated discussion in the parlor.

"You didn't *have* to go. You *chose* to go," Kitty whispered.

"I can't believe after all this time you are still acting this way. The man died. Murdered from what I understand," Judge replied.

"You know what they've been saying. And it will start all over again," Kitty said.

"I'm tired, Kitty. I'm going to wash up."

Becky realized now was not the time to talk to anyone. She'd never heard her parents speak to one another with such hostility.

"Just remember, Judge, I have invested just as much as you," Kitty said.

Becky ducked around the corner into the kitchen to make it look as if she was coming from that direction. With every step, she felt the sting of the blisters on her feet. Her father didn't see her. Unfortunately, Becky didn't see Fanny sitting in the kitchen. She should have known her cousin would be nearby if a whispered conversation was taking place.

"Looks like someone is doing a little snooping," Fanny said as she peeked into the pot of soup that was simmering on the stove.

The houseworkers, Moxley and Lucretia, had taken their son, Teeter, to the fair. They were probably having a grand time, eating frankfurters and popcorn and riding on the carousel, pulling off a gold ring with every round-a-bout. So they'd made supper early and just left it simmering. It would taste thick and flavorful, but Becky felt she had no stomach for it at all.

"If anyone knew what snooping looked like, it would be you," Becky said as if on cue.

"You can say whatever you want to me. I'm not the one who missed your father's show and made your mother have to explain to Mrs. Merriweather that she had no idea where her only daughter was," Fanny said before slinking out of the kitchen.

Becky stood there dumbfounded. If all of this drama was because Kitty had had to explain to Mrs. Busy-body Merriweather, then there was more of a reason for Becky to be offended. Why Kitty put so much stock in what other people thought Becky was sure she'd never know. With renewed confidence, she walked into the parlor to talk with Kitty as if nothing had happened.

"Mama, I am almost positive Teddy Rockdale will be going back to the fair tonight. I was going to go with him. Do you mind if I do?" she asked politely.

"I don't know if he'll be going. His father knew the Foxworthys too. They may try and be respectful and see to the *newly widowed Mrs. Foxworthy*." Kitty said those last four words as if they had thorns on them. Becky had never heard that kind of tone come from her mother.

"Mama, is something wrong?" Becky asked.

Kitty looked at her daughter with red-rimmed eyes as if she'd been holding back tears. Her lips were pinched together, and her chin was high in that silent, dignified way she had about her. She patted her hair into place, sniffled, and swallowed hard.

"No. I'm going to retire to the back porch. If your father is looking for me, tell him that is where I'll be." Kitty said the words as if she was giving directions to a cab driver.

Without knowing what else to do, Becky went upstairs and knocked on her father's door. He answered in the same sour mood as Kitty.

"Mama is out on the back porch," she said and

suddenly smelled fresh cologne. "Are you going out somewhere?"

"I am," he replied and looked at her like she was a pesky shoeshine boy.

"Where are you going? Can I come?" Becky asked as her way of apologizing again for missing his grand performance.

"No," Judge said and shut the bedroom door on his daughter.

Something was going on, and Becky didn't think it was just the fact that she'd missed the Jolly Corks show. She was trying her best to win her parents over again. How many times was she expected to say she was sorry?

After she'd been standing there for a few minutes, as if her feet had grown roots, Judge yanked his bedroom door wide open and let out a yelp.

"Why are you still standing here? You're becoming more and more like your cousin Fanny," he snapped. He stomped away in a fresh shirt and trousers and shined shoes, his Elks Club fez in his hand. His face was freshly shaved, and his hair was coated with pomade to make it slick and shiny.

Becky's mouth fell open. She wanted to shout back at him that she was not anything like Fanny, but he'd already disappeared down the stairs. Then she heard the front door slam and the car engine start. Becky rushed to her bedroom window, threw back the curtains, and watched as her father turned the car around and drove off.

He was going to the Elks Club. That explained why he was dressed nicely and smelled good. But something didn't sit right. Judge had never left the house with Kitty in a state like she was. Something was going on between them, and if it had come to the surface because of Becky's behavior earlier in the day, well, she wanted to know it. But it was obvious neither Kitty nor Judge was in any mood to talk to her. A visit to the Rockdale house was just what Becky needed.

After a delicious serving of Lucretia's soup with homemade bread and butter and a slice of homemade chocolate pie, Becky made a beeline to Teddy Rockdale's house. The well-worn path between the Mackenzies' plantation and the Rockdale estate had been established when she and Teddy were just children and would find their way back and forth between the properties several times a day. Not much had changed.

"Is that my favorite skirt coming down the path?" she heard Teddy shouting from the front porch.

"You better be talking about me and not Fanny," Becky replied as she swung her clutch purse on its thin chain strap.

Teddy shoved his hands into his pockets and rocked on his heels. He was already dressed in a sleek pair of trousers and two-toned shoes, along with a straw hat and a short, wide, bright-yellow tie.

"Of course not." Teddy shook his head. "She's ugly."

"Fiddlesticks. Even blind men see her walk by," Becky muttered as she made her way up the porch steps.

"That was some excitement at the fair," Teddy said as he handed Becky a mint julep from a tray of them sitting on a wicker table next to the porch swing.

"It was. That whole ordeal got me in a heap of trouble at home," Becky said as she sipped her drink. The air was still hot even though the sun had gone down, and barely any breeze had kicked up. The cool, sugary drink went down easy. Or maybe it just seemed that way as Becky told Teddy her woes.

"That's too bad, Beck. Parents are difficult animals," he replied before pulling a cigarette from his pocket and offering one to Becky. She happily accepted. A drink always seemed to go down better with a ciggy.

"He got all slicked up to go to the Elks Club tonight for the meeting. I guess they are all planning something for the Widow Foxworthy," Becky added as they rocked in the porch swing like they'd done since they were kids.

"There's no meeting of the Elks tonight," Teddy said.

"Of course there is. Daddy left in a fresh shirt with his hair combed and had his fez with him," Becky said before taking a sip, still looking at Teddy over the top of her silver cup.

"Nope. My dad is inside, fast asleep. Said to me that the Elks Club was going to meet in a week to discuss how to handle Foxworthy's death. He was their sergeant-at-arms. Now they need to replace him, and well, that is no easy task." Teddy shrugged.

"So why would my father say he was going to the Elks Club?" Becky asked as she recalled the ripple she'd witnessed between her mother and father and the words Kitty had said about the *newly widowed Mrs. Foxworthy*. The wheels started to turn, and in an instant, she reversed direction.

"I'm sure I don't know," Teddy replied.

"Do you know anything about Mrs. Foxworthy?" Becky asked.

Teddy let out a whistle. "She's got a lot of money."

"There are a lot of women who have a lot of money in Savannah. What else?" Becky pushed before taking another sip.

"Oh, you know how the rumor mill works, Rebecca. She's got a lot of money, but her family hails from Tennessee, so there must be more to the story." He rolled his eyes. "I just don't understand you women. If another female joins the mix who is rich or pretty or both, the claws come out." He made a scratching motion at Becky, making her roll *her own* eyes.

"Is Mrs. Foxworthy pretty?" Becky asked.

"I've heard she is. Truthfully, I've never seen her. Heard she's a bit of a homebody. At least, according to Mr. Foxworthy, she was. But I heard stories about him too. His accident today might not have been an accident," Teddy replied.

"What have you heard?" Becky scooted closer to Teddy and set down her cup in order to grab a fresh one.

"Well, according to some of the gents at the Elks Club, he was meeting up with some woman from the wrong side of the tracks at least once a week," Teddy said. "But I heard Mrs. Foxworthy had been up to no good too."

Becky rocked in the chair and studied the leaves of mint in her cup. "Teddy, let's go to the Elks Club."

"What for? There ain't nothing going on there. Trust me. If there was, my father would already be there. He never misses a meeting," Teddy insisted.

"Okay, well, if there isn't anything happening, then we'll go on over to the fair for a spell and see what's shakin'," Becky said.

"Now you're speaking my language. Shall we?" He offered Becky his arm, and within minutes, they were off.

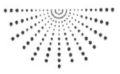

CHAPTER FOUR

*T*he Benevolent and Protective Order of the Elks Club building was a plain, square structure that looked as uninteresting as Becky thought it would. It was positioned on a small hill with a long, snaking driveway that led up to the parking area. She'd never been inside, as there was never any reason. This was a men's club. There was no need for frills or flowers. This was a place where they talked politics, discussed philosophies, and organized charity events that featured the Jolly Corks Vaudeville Show. Becky was pretty sure they had a rather well-stocked bar based on the number of times her father had come home lit after a meeting.

"See, I told you this place wasn't happening

tonight. My father never misses a meeting," Teddy said as he stopped the car before reaching the top of the long driveway.

"Park here. I want to take a closer look," Becky said.

"What for? This place is as dead as a doornail. Come on, Beck. The fair awaits. Games. Roasted franks. And I'm sure we can scare up some gin somewhere." Teddy clicked his tongue and winked.

"I promise. Just give me five minutes," Becky said as she hopped out of the car and hurried up to the top of the hill. There she saw her father's car and a few others that she didn't recognize. This was not the entire Elks Club in attendance. She was sure of that. Becky swallowed hard and looked at the dark building. Around the eastern side, she spotted a faint light in one of the windows. Carefully, she crept to it, stepping over two rakes, a shovel, and a hoe. On her most tippy tiptoes, she peeked into the window.

"This is a very serious situation," she heard one of the men say.

"I, for one, am not surprised this happened," another said.

"Now, Sid, we all know how you felt about Clem Foxworthy, but…"

"Don't *but* me, Arnie. Half the Elks felt the same

way. I know it isn't very Christian to speak ill of the dead, but the man had it coming. What did he think was going to happen? A man don't take kindly to another man courting his woman even if they are separated. It just ain't right," Sid said.

"Now, you know those were only rumors," Arnie replied.

"Arnie, I have to agree with Sid. They were more than rumors, and I don't know how it will look to the respectable people of town if we go on throwing a big event in his honor. Just because he was an Elk doesn't mean he walked on water."

Becky recognized that voice as belonging to Mr. Wolf. He had been at the Mackenzie plantation on more than one occasion to sip gin and reminisce with Judge about the things he used to do when he was a young man. He had been rough and tough in his youth, and although he was slower now, Becky didn't think much had changed.

"Wolfie, we aren't just talking about his memory. Bernice Foxworthy will benefit from a decent tribute, and the rumors might finally be put to rest," Arnie replied.

"Judge, what do you think?" Wolfie asked.

"I don't know if Judge is in a position to say anything. Sorry, Judge, but you have had your own dealings with Clem and Bernice. Especially Bernice. And I didn't want to say anything, but I don't know if you want any of that to come to light," Sid said.

Becky's heart stopped when she heard this. What was Sid talking about? What didn't her father want to come to light in regard to Bernice Foxworthy? She held her breath and listened.

"That was a long time ago, Sid," Judge said.

"I know. But we do know about it, and so does Bernice. And if she knows, you can bet there are some other ladies around town who know. I don't think it's anything you want floating to the surface," Sid said.

"What is it exactly that you think is going to float to the surface, Sid?" Judge snapped.

Just then, Teddy came tearing around the corner of the building, tripped over a root from a tree, and collided into the row of tools, making enough noise to rouse Mr. Foxworthy from the morgue in the middle of town. Becky quickly grabbed him by the hand, and they tore off into the darkness toward a toolshed, where the rakes and hoe should have been stored to begin with.

"What was that?" All the men inside crowded around the window just as Becky pulled Teddy into the shadows. She clapped a hand over his mouth, and they stood there stone still. She heard her father telling the other men he'd go check it out. A thin side door opened, and a shaft of light cut across the grass. His shadow came closer but stopped when the door to the shed opened up.

"Mr. Mackenzie?" It was a low, gravelly voice.

Becky, with her hand still over Teddy's mouth, peeked around the side of the shed. In the dim light from the door, she saw a familiar silhouette in addition to her father's.

"You've stuck to your part of the deal?" Judge asked.

"Yes, sir. You saw it for yourself," No-cent replied.

Becky watched as Judge reached into his pocket and pulled out a folded envelope and handed it to the rummy.

"Now get out of town. There's a train leaving at midnight," Judge said.

"Are you sure you don't want me to stick around? In case you need another one done?" No-cent asked, his voice so low that it was as if he were slithering on the ground like a snake.

"Be on that train," Judge ordered before going back inside and shutting the side door tightly.

Becky didn't look at Teddy, who was patiently standing there with her hand on his mouth.

Quietly, No-cent cut across the grass in the opposite direction of the driveway and slipped into the line of trees. Becky had no desire to follow him this time. In fact, she felt rather sick to her stomach.

"Did you hear that?" she whispered to Teddy as she pulled her hand away from his mouth.

"No. What was it? Who was there?" Teddy asked.

Becky choked the words back and shook her head. "Uh, I don't know. I could barely hear them. You were right. There isn't anything big going on here. Let's go home."

"Home? After you dragged me all the way out here? No way. We're going to the fair. Besides, Martha will be there, and I think there will be a tall glass of water waiting for you."

Teddy took his best friend by the hand and casually strolled across the grounds, safely away from the window and back down the drive toward his car. They were gone without anyone noticing. But Becky's mind was whirling as if she was on one of those rides that spun around so fast that people stuck to the wall. Her stomach was upset, and her heart broke every time she thought of what those men had said to her father. What was Judge trying to hide? Did it have something to do with the newly widowed Bernice Foxworthy?

As they reached the fair, Becky had hoped all the bright lights and the night owls in attendance would have cheered her up a little. Instead, they made her feel worse, and she couldn't think of any place she wanted less to be. She wanted to go home. But she'd promised Teddy, and he was a good sport all night long.

"Come on. Martha is bound to be around here somewhere," Teddy said as he hopped out of his car and got the door for Becky. "Hey, you don't seem like yourself. What's eating you, Beck?"

"Nothing a stiff drink can't help." She forced a smile and took Teddy's hand. He winked at her, helped her from the car, and slipped his arm around her waist as they walked into the fair in a hunt to find Martha. Becky hoped they'd find her quickly.

As if by magic, she spotted her in the one place Becky didn't want to go: the fortune-teller's tent.

CHAPTER FIVE

"There she is!" Teddy pointed and led Becky to the tent that seemed to have been the starting point of all her troubles that day.

Thankfully, Madame Cecelia wasn't the one gazing into the crystal ball. It was Ophelia, her mother. The woman was dressed in all black and managed to blend into the shadows that all but consumed the inside of the tent. There were a few lanterns around that gave the place a mystical, eerie glow, and all of it was amplified by Ophelia's stark-white hair and her one blind white eye.

"Well, look what the cat dragged in," Martha squealed happily, only to get a stern glare from Ophelia. "Sorry, Miss Ophelia."

"Is okay. We are through. You like to have your fortune read?" She looked up at Teddy.

"No thanks. I already know my future. I'm going to have the prettiest girl on my arm for the rest of the evening," he said as he released Becky and took Martha's hand.

"My hero," Martha gushed and batted her eyes at him before giving him a quick peck on the cheek.

"Rebecca. Come and sit," Ophelia almost ordered her to do so.

"No. I already had my fortune told this afternoon," Becky replied, forcing a smile.

"I know that. A lot has changed since then." Ophelia gestured toward the chair, but Becky was sure it was rigged with electricity, and if she took a seat, she'd be fried like a convict at Alcatraz. She shook her head.

"There is heartbreak ahead. But you'll be better off."

Ophelia's cryptic message didn't help her at all. In fact, it made her feel worse. She squinted at the old woman, who had never, in all the time Becky had known her, ever smiled. Now was no exception. She stared at Becky, her milky eye blind yet still seeing, and nodded.

"I thought I'd find you here," a familiar voice said

from behind Becky, making her instantly feel better. She turned around and looked up about twelve inches to see the handsome face of Adam White, her Yankee beau.

"Aren't you a sight for sore eyes." Becky let out her breath as if she'd been under water for days. "Thanks, Ophelia. I'll stop by the shop."

Ophelia nodded and proceeded to pull out the same deck of tarot cards that Cecelia had used earlier in the day. The last thing Becky wanted was to have a repeat of that ordeal. She slipped her hand into Adam's and quickly pulled him from the fortune-teller tent.

"You wouldn't believe the day I've had," she said as she and Adam walked behind Martha and Teddy.

"That bad, huh?" Adam looked down at her, his dark curly hair falling lazily over his forehead and his blue eyes twinkling in the bright carnival lights.

"Yeah. I think..." She stopped herself from speaking. Did she dare utter the words that had been sinking deeper and deeper into her brain? That her father had been doing something he shouldn't have been. That Madame Cecelia had told her someone would be leaving her, but she never, ever expected it to be her father. That he might have had something to do with the death of Clem Foxworthy. It was all just too much, and it showed itself as tears in her eyes.

"Beck? Becky, honey, what's wrong?" Adam asked.

"It's just been a bad day. That's all. I'm just…ready to forget everything for a while and look at it new with the sun tomorrow." She managed a smile. "Come on. Teddy and Martha are getting away from us."

She couldn't tell him what she was thinking. She didn't dare tell him about what she had heard and seen with her own eyes during her father's exchange with No-cent. Anyone with any decency didn't rub elbows with that kind of riffraff. Especially not the very successful tobacco farmer Judge Mackenzie. No, Becky kept it all to herself.

That night, they went on the carousel. Becky found herself a seahorse, and Adam was next to her on a roaring lion. The music was loud enough to drown out all of Becky's thoughts, and when Teddy passed around his flask, the nip was enough to calm her nerves.

After the carousel, they went into the row of games, where the barkers, combined with the sounds of the rides and the loud laughter of the crowd, made Becky forget her troubles. Although the horrible thought kept lingering around the edge of her mind and peeked at her like a shy child through a staircase bannister, she managed to keep it from fully appearing in the middle of her thoughts and ruining her good time.

Adam won her a funny-looking stuffed monkey in a red vest with black button eyes after he brought a heavy mallet down on the strong man's challenge and rang the bell.

"I'll name him Adam," Becky teased as they slowly walked behind Teddy and Martha, who were sharing a bag of peanuts.

"Yeah, well, I can sort of see the resemblance," Adam said as he looked at the toy in her arms. "Tell me, are you feeling better?"

"Yes." Becky was telling the truth. She was feeling better. She was sure it was just all the excitement from the night, but it was exactly what she'd needed. All the things she had to sort out would be there tomorrow. After the day she'd had, it was intoxicating to be with people who were genuinely happy she was there.

Adam took her hand and pulled her between two tents. It was dark. Becky liked how the shadow fell over Adam's face and made him look mysterious and even bigger and stronger than he already was. His calloused hand came to her face and gently pushed her hair back while stroking her soft cheek. When she put her hands on his chest, she could feel his heart beating as wildly as hers. With the laughter from the games and the screams from the rides in the background, Becky lifted her chin to meet Adam's soft lips. They kissed as the carnival noises swirled around them. She could have stayed there until the sun came up. When Adam pulled back from her and she looked up, his eyes were still closed. When they opened, he looked at her seriously.

"Marry me, Becky."

"What?"

"You heard me. Marry me. Let's hop in my car and drive all night until the sun comes up. Then we'll find a justice of the peace in some little town and get married," Adam said before licking his lips and swallowing hard.

This was not how Becky had envisioned getting engaged. She had thought there would be the ceremonial request for permission from her father, and a ring would be presented. Not on a hot night in between two tents.

"Adam, I don't know," Becky stammered.

"Don't you love me?"

"Of course I do. Adam, I love you more than

anything. But I can't just rush off and elope. It would break my mother's heart," Becky replied. "I don't think I need to explain to you the etiquette of a proper Southern engagement. You can imagine the scandal if I breeched that."

Adam tilted his head to the left and took Becky's hands in his. "I think you're just nervous. I sprang this on you too quickly, and I spooked you. How about a week from today, we go get hitched?"

"Adam, I can't just rush off like that. It isn't how a wedding is done," Becky protested.

"I'm not talking about a wedding. I'm talking about marriage. You and me. That doesn't involve anyone else," he said, holding his hands up to his heart.

"Can we talk about this tomorrow? Can I have a night to think about it and make a plan?" Becky asked and watched as Adam looked away then back at her.

He smiled and smoothed her wavy red hair. "Okay, think about it tonight. Then I'll call on you tomorrow, and we'll make our plans." He winked as if the problem had been resolved.

Becky felt a knot form in her stomach as they slipped out from between the tents and caught up to

Martha and Teddy, who had barely noticed they were missing.

"What do you two say about heading over to Willie's for a nightcap?" Teddy asked as they made their way toward the exit.

"I think that sounds delightful," Martha said. "I feel like we haven't had a chance to talk all night, Becky. Where's Fanny?"

"I left her at home. She and my mother have become the best of friends, so I didn't think there was a need to bring her with," Becky replied without the slightest concern for hiding the anger in her voice.

"Uh-oh. Sounds like something happened. Spill," Martha ordered as she let go of Teddy's hand and slipped her arm through Becky's.

As they got to the car, Teddy said he'd drive. Adam offered to meet them there but said he had to make a stop first, and he urged Becky to go with Martha.

"Are you sure?" Becky asked Adam. He smiled happily.

"I am. You go ahead, and I'll be at Willie's before you have your first dance." He winked at her, making her heart jump before he climbed into his car and pulled away.

Becky finished telling Martha everything that had happened with Fanny. She left out the part about Madame Cecelia's tarot reading and the terrible truth she was afraid was happening with her father. She also didn't mention a word about Adam's proposal. That was just one too many things that had happened that day, and only a crazy person would repeat them all.

When they finally got to Willie's, they were underdressed and overdue for a couple of drinks and a few dances. They'd been there for about an hour before Becky realized that Adam hadn't come back.

CHAPTER SIX

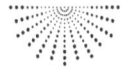

*T*he next day, Becky came downstairs with a throbbing headache. Unfortunately, it had nothing to do with being hungover. At least then she'd know that a healthy breakfast and some strong coffee would put her upright again. This was a headache from the hullabaloo that had chased her around all day yesterday. It had all started with that darn Clem Foxworthy up and choking to death. If only Becky had arrived at the fair five minutes later, the whole thing could have been avoided. Then she would have never followed Vincent No-cent, and she would have never missed her father's show, and Kitty wouldn't be drawing up the adoption papers for Fanny to replace her as her one and only daughter.

When she sat down at the dining room table, not much had changed. Except when Becky looked at her father, he kept his face behind the newspaper.

"Good morning," she said as if she was trying not to wake a five-hundred-pound gorilla.

"Good morning, Rebecca," Kitty said and barely looked up from a book she was reading. If her mother was still calling her Rebecca, Becky knew she was still in the doghouse.

"Hi, Daddy. Anything interesting in the paper?" Becky hoped to get a better reply from him, but that was short-lived.

"Not really," he said. He quickly folded the newspaper, stood from the table, and took one last sip of coffee. He said he was going out to tend the fields and would be heading into town for most of the day.

Becky swallowed hard as she looked at her mother, who barely moved an inch and kept her eyes on the book in front of her while taking a sip of coffee.

Just then, Fanny appeared. She wearing a terribly bright-pink dress that upset Becky's already throbbing head.

"Good morning," she chirped. "I could have slept another three hours for sure. I think all that fuss and being in the hot sun yesterday plum tuckered me out."

"Have some coffee, Fanny," Kitty replied without looking up.

Becky wanted to ask her mother what the matter was, but if she was fixing to give her another dressing down over her bad manners the day before, she just wasn't up for it. So she kept her mouth quiet.

"Don't mind if I do," Fanny said as she picked up the paper Judge had left behind and began to scan the articles. "Did you see this? The police said that man who died at the pie contest was poisoned."

"What?" Becky's heart dropped.

"Says so right here. After further investigation, it was determined by the county coroner that Mr. Clemont Willis Foxworthy was poisoned. Funny the fellow being poisoned just as he was judging a pie contest." Fanny shook her head and handed the paper to Becky.

She snatched it quickly from her cousin and read the entire article. She touched her temple tenderly as the pain started to subside. If Mr. Foxworthy had been poisoned and he was not well liked, as Arnie and Sid had said the previous night, maybe her father wasn't as involved as she'd thought.

"This is great news," Becky gasped, causing her

mother and Cousin Fanny to look at her as if she just started to pick her nose at the table.

"What?" Fanny gasped.

"No. I don't mean about Mr. Foxworthy. I meant about this other article here. See? They are fixing to dedicate the corner of Blakely and Pine to Caldonia Mae Richmond for her charity work with United Pilgrims for the Poor. See? Right here." Becky pointed to the tiny blurb in the corner. Then she cleared her throat.

Lucretia came into the kitchen with the hot silver pot of steaming coffee and poured both Becky and Fanny a cup.

"Did you enjoy the fair last night, Lucy?" Becky asked, hoping the cold shoulder she'd been receiving from everyone else in the Mackenzie home hadn't spread to Lucretia and Moxley.

"Oh, we had a fine time, thank you, Miss Becky," Lucy replied as she poured.

"Good thing you didn't go with us. I'm sure you heard about the pie contest." Becky tapped the paper.

"I did," she replied. She smiled and hurried back into the kitchen. Becky looked at Fanny, who was inspecting her reflection in a butter knife. Kitty appeared to be reading. Becky shrugged, grabbed her cup of coffee, and went into the kitchen.

"Lucretia? Did you hear something interesting about the pie contest?" Becky asked as she took a sip of her coffee.

"Miss Becky, that was a terrible thing that happened to Mr. Foxworthy. But when I heard what the people were saying about him, I think that was worse," Lucretia said. "Especially George Dover."

"George Dover. Daddy's friend?" Becky asked in a hushed voice. "They're all Elks. What could George have to say about the man?"

"He came by here last night. After your father got home from his errand. He showed up here drunk, crying and cussing out Mr. Foxworthy as if the man hadn't died in front of a mob of people. It was down-right disrespectful." Lucretia shook her head.

"Did he say why he was so upset?" Becky asked, still keeping her voice low.

"He said that Mr. Foxworthy was making fun of him for submitting a pie to the contest," Lucretia whispered. "I heard from Mr. Dover's maid, Lil, that he'd been baking for weeks to make sure he had the perfect blueberry pie. But as it got closer to the contest, he was getting more and more nervous because Mr. Foxworthy had been chosen to be the judge."

"Really?" Becky couldn't have been happier to

hear this news. If Mr. Dover had had an ax to grind with Mr. Foxworthy and had put poison in his own pie to even the score, that meant her daddy didn't have anything to do with his death.

"Lil told me last night when I saw her at the fair that Mr. Dover was celebrating. She got out of the house and planned to stay out until all the lights were off, even if that meant sleeping on the back porch," Lucretia added.

Just then, her son Teeter came inside, his teeth bright as he smiled.

"Hi, Miss Becky!" he said as he dashed into Becky's arms as if he hadn't seen her in years.

"Howdy-do, Teeter. You know how much I love hugs. What have you been up to?" Becky asked as she squeezed the boy back.

"My daddy's teaching me to read," he said proudly. "We're reading *Treasure Island*. It's so exciting!"

"That's one of my favorites," Becky said, running her hand over his soft black hair. "You tell me when you finish, and then I'll read you *Tarzan of the Jungle*."

"You promise?" Teeter's eyes were wide with excitement.

He loved spending time with Becky and vice versa.

There was something special about Teeter that Becky had taken a shine to since the day he was born. If she ever got married and had children, she'd pray for a boy just like him: barefoot all the time, chasing life down every dusty path or into every puddle of rainwater.

Just then, the thought of marriage just about slapped her across the face, and she remembered what Adam had said to her last night.

"Cross my heart," Becky said.

Teeter gave her one more squeeze then ran to tell his father, who was out tending to the mailbox, which had become slightly wobbly.

"Miss Becky, are you having any breakfast today?" Lucretia asked.

"Just the coffee," Becky said as she poured herself another cup. "Thanks for the scoop on Mr. Foxworthy and Mr. Dover."

"Chills my bones just to think about it," Lucretia said as she finished cooking four slices of French toast for Fanny.

Becky went back to the dining room with her cup of coffee and was about to head back upstairs to change her clothes when her mother cleared her throat.

"Becky, your father and I don't want you going to

the fair this evening—or for the rest of the week for that matter," Kitty said.

"What? Why? Everyone is going to be there. And the firecrackers are scheduled for Friday. We always go see the fireworks." Becky looked at her mother with wide eyes.

"Things are different this year. I don't want to discuss it any further," Kitty said.

"Mama, I apologized the best I know how. If Mrs. Merriweather has something to say to you, I'll go apologize to her too. But please don't make us miss the fireworks." Becky was torn between stomping her feet like a child and trying to reason like an adult. She was angry. Never in her life had she felt her parents were being downright mean to her. She'd made mistakes before, but never had her entire world been turned upside down over it.

"This has nothing to do with Mrs. Merriweather. This has to do with my daughter needing to learn responsibility," Kitty said as she stood from the table.

"What about Fanny? You're going to relegate her to the property too?" Becky huffed.

"Fanny isn't my child. She may come and go as she pleases. You are my daughter. And if I say you're not to go to the fair, then you are not to go. If you are having a problem with that, then I suggest you talk to your father." Kitty walked past Becky and out of the room.

"What is going on?" Becky looked at her cousin, who remained in her seat.

A few seconds went by, and then Lucretia brought Fanny her breakfast. The argument at the table hadn't affected her appetite.

"Maybe Aunt Kitty just needs to rest a while," Fanny said.

"Easy for you to say," Becky muttered angrily.

"Cousin Becky, can I give you some advice?" Fanny said after swallowing a mouthful of French toast.

"No."

"You may not like to hear this, but..." Fanny started.

"Did you not hear me?" Becky snapped.

"For once, do what your parents are asking. It's just a fair. There will be another one next year," Fanny said.

This was perfect for Fanny. She'd have Teddy and Martha and Adam all to herself. Especially Adam. Once again, his proposal of marriage popped into Becky's mind, and she felt her chest tighten. Not a single retort came to her, so she left. This was too much.

Well, Kitty Mackenzie might have told Becky to stay away from the fair, but she hadn't told her she had to stay home. Once upstairs in her room, Becky changed into a pretty, lightweight brown skirt and a billowy blouse that was perfect for the hot weather.

Everything in her life had changed when Mr. Foxworthy died. And if the newspaper said it was murder, then Becky was going to find out who'd had it in for the man. She'd stay away from the fair. But she wasn't going to stay in, and she purposefully let the front screen door slam shut when she left.

CHAPTER SEVEN

*G*eorge Dover was a bearlike man. He was tall, rounded at the shoulders, and took short steps when he walked. She was sure that with one swat, he could easily lay a fellow out. It was rather funny that he had had an entry in the pie contest. He looked like he'd have been comfortable running the dunk tank or maybe the giant scale where he'd guess people's weight.

He didn't look like someone who would bake a dainty blueberry pie. So he made a rather easy target for Clem Foxworthy to pick on. But was that enough to kill a man? Becky looked down at the paper she'd written his address on. Before she'd left her house in a huff, she snuck into her father's office and, after rummaging through his desk, found the directory of Elks Club members. It took her about twenty minutes to walk, but that gave her time to drum up a reason for paying him a visit.

Mr. Dover lived on a small pecan farm. There was a rumor around town that he'd been married at one time but that his wife had left him for unknown reasons. But that was ancient history. The pecan farm wasn't nearly as grand as the Mackenzie plantation, but it was well-known, and as Becky hiked up the long driveway, she noticed the heavy smell of pecans from the trees that stood like guards all the way up to the house.

The farmhouse was a faded red with beautiful wildflowers growing around it. Just as she was about to step onto the porch, a deep voice caught her attention.

"Can I help you, gal?"

Becky whirled around and saw Mr. Dover standing with a rake in his hand. His jalopy was in front of the barn, and Becky was positive it had been at the Elks Club the night before.

"Hi, Mr. Dover. It's me, Becky Mackenzie?" she said politely before slowly taking a couple steps toward him.

"Oh, hello, Becky. I barely recognized you. My

goodness. The last time I saw you, I think you were wearing your hair in pigtails." He smiled.

"Yes, sir. That's probably right." Becky chuckled.

"What can I do for you, honey?"

"Well, you were in such a state last night that I was worried about you. So I thought I'd just pay you a visit to see if you were feeling better." She smiled as sweetly as she could, tilting her head to the right and clasping her hands in front of her.

In an instant, Mr. Dover's demeanor changed. "You were home last night? I didn't see you there. Judge said everyone was in bed." He looked embarrassed and angry.

"He probably didn't know, but I sometimes sneak up the trellis to get into my room when I'm arriving home late so as not to disturb anyone." Becky shrugged, hoping her exchange of a secret would put Mr. Dover at ease.

His shoulders sagged a little, and he seemed to relax. "Well, I am sorry about disturbing you, Becky. I wasn't myself last night," he admitted.

"It's quite all right. Especially under the circumstances. Mr. Foxworthy's accident was terribly shocking to everyone." Becky hoped if she opened the door a crack, Mr. Dover would walk right in.

"I'm sure you heard what I said about Mr.

Foxworthy." Mr. Dover hung his head. "I didn't mean it. Or maybe I did. He was not a kind man." Becky stood there as Mr. Dover stared at the ground for a few seconds. "I can't help but think the world is better off without the likes of Clem Foxworthy."

"Did he hurt you, Mr. Dover?" Becky asked before she even realized the question had formed in her head.

Mr. Dover chuckled bitterly and jerked his head toward the porch before starting to walk in that direction. Becky followed.

"I'm sure your daddy has told you that being part of the Benevolent and Protective Order of the Elks Club isn't being a member of just any club. We take our oath seriously. We strive to be good, decent men. Well, Clem Foxworthy wasn't fit to shine the shoes of the lowliest member of the Elks Club. Yet he thought he was the grand poohbah."

Becky had to take two steps for each one of Mr. Dover's.

"My. Something smells delicious," Becky said as she stepped into the kitchen behind Mr. Dover.

"I'm baking another pie. This one is for myself. Sort of a celebratory pie. I didn't lose the pie-baking contest after all." He smiled innocently as he shrugged. "I love to bake. Do you find it strange that a man like me likes to bake?"

"Not at all. I'd think it would be quite an admirable quality for a man to have," she said without explaining her own inability to even boil water.

"I tried to like Clem. I did. But he just made it impossible. He voted against everything I was in favor of. I wanted to deliver balloons to the patients at the hospital, since they couldn't attend the fair. He made sure that was voted down. At Christmas last year, I thought it would have been nice to dedicate a large tree to those who fell in the war. He rallied to make sure we didn't have enough funds for that. It seemed no matter what I suggested, he was against it," Mr. Dover said as he walked over to the oven.

Part of her wanted to stay on the porch, but Mr. Dover was talking freely. He might clam up at any second. The house was cozy, clean, and simply decorated, with no sign of any feminine touches aside from one picture that Becky squinted to see. It looked like a wedding picture, but she couldn't be sure and didn't want to appear nosey—even though that was exactly what she was.

"Some people are like that," Becky replied, thinking of Fanny.

Mr. Dover went to the icebox and grabbed a pitcher of water. He took a small jelly jar from a tall shelf and poured a glass, handing it to Becky, who was grateful for the drink.

"I'm not a violent person. That's what I told your father, as I'm sure you heard. But I was just so tired of Clem. My hobby is precious to me. And when he said he didn't care if my blueberry pie tasted best of all, that he'd never give me a blue ribbon, I don't know what came over me."

Becky's heart seized, and she stopped in mid-drink, her eyes wide with the sudden downpour of information. She had no idea what he was talking about. But she couldn't help but try and smile supportively.

"What kind of man talks in such a manner? If I'd done something to him, I could understand his hostility, but I hadn't. Up until that day." Mr. Dover pinched his lips together and poured himself a glass of water.

"That's terrible. I'm really sorry," Becky said as she watched the hulking man stand there in front of his icebox, looking sad and unwanted.

"Well, thank you. But I take comfort in knowing that what goes around does come around. Finally, an opportunity for Foxworthy to get his comeuppance presented itself, and someone took it. He was murdered, you know," Mr. Dover said before taking a long drink.

"That's what the paper said this morning," Becky replied before setting her glass down on the kitchen table.

She looked at the quaint shelf behind Mr. Dover's head and felt her entire body freeze over. She'd spied a simple brown bottle with a peeling label. But the words Strych-Nine Nitrate might as well have been under a spotlight.

Mr. Dover chuckled. "It's already in the paper?"

"Yes." Becky swallowed hard.

"Hmm. Did you see anything about the pie-baking contest being rescheduled at the fair?" he asked absently.

"I'm sorry to have bothered you, Mr. Dover. I'd best be on my way. If there is anything you need from my father, please…" Becky backed up a step, but Mr. Dover frowned at her and set his glass down.

"I sure would enjoy another chance to showcase my pies. Now that everyone knows my secret, it would be nice to share it." He winked at Becky.

"Yes, sir. Well, perhaps there will be something at the church. They are always looking for good desserts to auction," Becky suggested as she took a step toward the door.

"If you wait, you can have a slice. You won't want another pie after you taste mine. Trust me, you'll think you died and went to heaven." Mr. Dover's words sent chills up Becky's spine.

"I'd love to, Mr. Dover. But I have to be getting back. Daddy's waiting for me. We're supposed to go into town together." She backed up another step. "Would you like me to give him a message?"

"No," he replied before taking one long stride in Becky's direction.

Without waiting for him to get any closer, Becky shouted another good-bye as she bolted out the door and down the porch steps. In a flurry of dust, she practically ran down the dirt path toward the main road, hoping she'd be able to hop on the back of some farmer's truck to take her in any direction away from Mr. Dover's farm.

Within just a few minutes, as Becky turned and looked over her shoulder, half expecting Mr. Dover to be lumbering after her with a fork in one hand and a plate of blueberry pie in the other, a truck appeared. She smiled as best she could and waved.

"Need a lift, missy?"

"Sure do," she huffed and smiled gratefully at the gray-haired man with crooked teeth and bib over-alls. Next to him was a small boy in similar bibs with similar crooked teeth. It was obvious Grandpa was taking his grandson out on an errand.

He jerked his thumb over his shoulder. "Climb in."

Becky ran around the back of the truck and got into the open bed, her feet dangling over the edge. She pounded the side to let the old man know she was safely on board, and away they went. As Becky watched the fields go by, she wondered what she'd just escaped. Could Mr. Dover have poisoned Mr. Foxworthy? He did have poison right there in his kitchen. He did say some rather incriminating things to Judge the night before. Well, maybe not incrimi-nating, but they were suspicious, according to Lucretia.

Yes. He had something to do with it. He had to. That meant Judge had nothing to do with it, and there was just a little hullabaloo between the Mackenzie family members. If she were sweeter than sugar, she'd get everyone back into good spirits. She was sure of it. And if that included being pleasant to Fanny, Becky was willing to do it. She swallowed hard and wasn't sure if it was the dust in her throat that tasted bitter or the idea of chumming up to Fanny.

CHAPTER EIGHT

When Becky finally arrived home, her father hadn't returned, and Kitty was bustling around the house like a dandelion spore in the wind.

"Hi, Mama. What are you doing?" Becky asked before giving her mother a peck on the cheek.

"What in the world have you been up to, child? You're filthy," Kitty exclaimed, stepping back from Becky as if she was covered in black soot from a coal mine.

"Oh, well, I got into a tussle with a raccoon over a peach I'd picked from the tree down by the cemetery. That masked bandit will think twice about trying to steal a peach from me again." Becky clasped her hands behind her back and rocked on her heels.

But her mother only shook her head. "I don't have time for your shenanigans. I'm sure you've forgotten that the women's auxiliary is gathering here this week for the monthly meeting." Kitty huffed. "And we've got two more members. Joelle Beuhler and Kerry Merriweather, Mrs. Merriweather's niece, have joined. I just don't know how we are all going to fit. We were snug like sardines the last time everyone was here."

Becky shrugged. "I wouldn't worry, Mama. Our house is plenty big enough. In fact, maybe the ladies would enjoy an afternoon outside? We've got the picnic tables that could be put together under the willows. You'd have plenty of room, and I don't think it would be a fuss for Lucretia and Daisy to go back and forth from the kitchen. And I'll bet..."

"And what if it rains?" Kitty snapped.

Becky stood there like she'd been slapped. Her mother had never talked to her this way before. Her heart instantly broke. She wanted to snap back but couldn't. This was her mother, and she had hurt her feelings by missing the Jolly Corks show. She'd also embarrassed her in front of Mrs. Merriweather, according to Fanny. Mr. Foxworthy wasn't the only one getting some comeuppance.

Just then, Fanny appeared.

"Aunt Kitty, do you have any plans on going into town? I'm just desperate for a new pair of stockings." She looked Becky up and down. "Why, Cousin Becky, you look like you danced with a dust devil."

Becky felt a quick retort charge up her throat, but she choked it back and shook her head. "If you all are going into town, I'd like to tag along."

"Yes. I do need to gather a few things for the luncheon. But Becky, I refuse to take you anywhere looking like you just crawled through a trench with Cobb's Legion. Go get cleaned up, and make it snappy," Kitty said.

"Yes, ma'am," Becky replied before dashing upstairs.

It didn't take long for her to change her clothes. She grabbed her purse and tried to choke down her emotions in order to make her mother feel better. Moxley was playing chauffeur today. As he drove, Kitty read off a list of the things she needed and asked Becky and Fanny if they'd help.

"Sure, Mama," Becky said, taking part of the list and handing the other part to Fanny. "We'll be done in a jiffy."

"Fine. We'll all meet back in front of the bank in one hour. Don't be late," Kitty said, looking at Becky.

"I bet I'll beat both of you back here with time to spare," Becky replied as she climbed out of the car.

The excitement and bustle of downtown always lifted her spirits. Everyone was hurrying to go one place or another. And Becky had to admit that she enjoyed the occasional whistle that came her way from the blokes eating their lunches on the sidewalk or a couple of gents in suits returning from a three-martini meeting. Fanny was probably causing cars to collide at the corners and fellas to fall off the curbs into traffic. But Becky was away from Fanny at the moment and glad for it.

The first thing on the list was the dry cleaning. Becky had been in Conway's Dry Cleaning a million times. It was just down to the end of the block and over two more. As she walked, she looked in the windows of the stores and thought about Mr. Dover. What was she going to do with the information she had? Should she go to the police? Maybe she should talk to her father first? But how was she going to do that without getting Lucretia in trouble for repeating what she'd heard? Perhaps a little white lie was in order. She could just tell Judge that she'd happened to cross paths with Mr. Dover. But just as she was figuring out the details of her fib, a ruckus grabbed her attention.

"I'll never speak to you again!" It was Mrs. Brower, one of the women who would be at Becky's house for her mother's ladies' auxiliary luncheon meeting. Her face was red as a beet, and she was pointing.

"That will be too soon!" replied Mrs. Hindergast, another member of the ladies' auxiliary, who was on the receiving end of Mrs. Brower's accusatory finger. "You stole my recipe, and you know you did! I told you this would be the last pie contest you'd ever enter!"

"Is that a threat, Tilly Hindergast?"

"It is, Caroline Brower! You mark my words! They don't allow baking in Sing Sing!"

Tilly Hindergast turned and stomped down the sidewalk. She was the kind of woman who looked like she baked pies. Her hips were wide in order to support a more-than-ample bosom. She wore her hair twisted in a tight bun on the top of her head, and her face was pulled just as tightly to the sides. She and Mrs. Brower had a feud going back at least a decade, with more vinegar between the two of them than the Hatfields and McCoys.

This recent altercation was one in a long line of furious accusations and arguments. They competed every spring over the best flower garden in Savannah. In September would come the judgment over who had the most perfect pumpkins. Christmas brought a cookie sale to help those less fortunate members of Savannah society, and Becky was sure she might have missed an occasion or two in between. Sometimes Mrs. Brower won. Sometimes Mrs. Hindergast won. But neither woman believed the other had ever won on merit. She'd cheated, connived, bribed, or stolen the blue ribbon in one way or another. And every year, there would be at least one public display of hostility between the two.

"Mrs. Hindergast, are you all right?" Becky asked as the woman nearly ran her over.

"Oh, Rebecca Mackenzie." She looked Becky up and down as if she were making sure they weren't wearing the same outfit. The chance of that was between slim and none, and slim had left town.

"What's going on?" Becky asked, paying no mind to the judgmental once-over.

"That Caroline Brower has always hated me. I can't help it that I've won more blue ribbons for my pies than she has." Tilly Hindergast pulled a kerchief from her purse and dabbed it all over her face and neck.

"This is about the pies?" Becky asked.

"Well, what else would it be about? She stole my

recipe. And I just know she did something to my pie this year. I was poised to win for the fourth year in a row, and she just couldn't let that happen," Mrs. Hindergast hissed.

"What do you think she did?" Becky asked as she clutched her own purse nervously.

"Why, Rebecca, where have you been? It's all over town that the judge, Clem Foxworthy, was poisoned," Tilly replied and looked at Becky as if she should have donned a dunce cap.

"You think she poisoned the pie?" Becky choked the words out.

"Most certainly she did. Of course, with her son-in-law being on the police force, she probably won't ever be brought to justice," Mrs. Hindergast replied as she tucked her kerchief back into her purse.

"That's a very serious accusation. Her reputation could be ruined if people heard you saying that she put poison in her blueberry pie," Becky pointed out.

"Oh, I don't believe she poisoned her *own* pie. She'd never get the blue ribbon then. She'd have to put it in *my* pie. That's the only way she'd win the contest." Mrs. Hindergast looked down her flat pug nose at Becky. "I was the *only* serious competition there."

"You don't really think she'd do that for a blue

ribbon?" Becky asked with her hand to her throat.

"No. Of course *she* wouldn't." Mrs. Hindergast smiled devilishly. "She'd have someone else do it for her. Someone would have to have snuck in there and done it. Someone no one would ever think twice about."

Becky remembered No-cent slipping out of the judging tent just before Mr. Foxworthy collapsed. Then he had tossed something into the pond. Could Mrs. Hindergast be on to something? But if what she was saying was true, why had her father given No-cent money and told him to leave town? Was it really just to help Mrs. Brower win a pie contest? It didn't sound on the up-and-up.

"But Mrs. Hindergast, you are suggesting that Mrs. Brower was willing to commit murder just to win a pie-baking contest. Can you see how that sounds rather…extraordinary?" Becky waited for Mrs. Hindergast to come to her senses, but instead, the other woman sneered at her.

"I wouldn't expect someone like yourself to understand. Not when slipping into every speakeasy in town is your hobby, along with turning down every decent fellow your mama has ever introduced to you." Mrs. Hindergast stood there stiffly, as if the elastic in her slip had suddenly given out.

"What did you just say?" Becky gasped.

"I said I wouldn't expect someone like you to understand if you hadn't spent any time perfecting family recipes and collecting the finest ingredients from several counties, only to find someone stole it and claimed it to be her own," Mrs. Hindergast replied, again looking at Becky as if she'd just seen some of her brain fall out of her head and onto the ground.

"Oh, uh, yes. Of course," Becky stuttered.

"Caroline Brower is a bitter, ruthless woman. Don't you forget it. If all the pies hadn't fallen together, I'd be behind bars, and my reputation for baking Savannah's finest pies four years in a row would be ruined," Mrs. Hindergast said before she left Becky standing on the sidewalk, staring after her.

Becky wasn't sure what had just happened. It was strange enough that Mrs. Hindergast was so convinced Mrs. Brower had intentionally poisoned her pie to win the baking contest. But she was positive she'd heard her criticize Becky's social life.

"You didn't eat anything this morning, Becky. You're out in the hot sun, running around. It's a wonder you don't have heat stroke," she muttered as she slowly started to walk along the sidewalk.

Her mind drifted, and she wondered if she should chase down Mrs. Brower and see what she had to say. But then she remembered the dry cleaning.

She gasped and dashed off to Conway's Dry Cleaning. Of course, since Becky was in a hurry, there were half a dozen people ahead of her. Finally, she got her father's suit. Without looking, she dashed out of the storefront and collided into a man in coveralls that were stained with grease. She dropped her father's suit on the ground, and the cuff of his pant leg fell into a puddle.

"I'm sorry, miss," the man said and graciously bent down to pick up the suit with hands also spotted with grease.

"No need to apologize. It was my fault for not looking where I was going." She quickly snatched the garment before he could touch it. With as pleasant a smile as she could muster, she folded the suit over her arm. "By now."

She hurried down the street, got confused, and made a wrong turn, going left when she should have gone right. All the while, her conversation with Mrs. Hindergast rolled around in her head like a marble in a bowl. When she finally arrived in front of the bank, Kitty and Fanny were already there.

"Hey!" Becky waved cheerfully.

"Well, it's about time," Fanny said. "Had I known I was going to be standing around all afternoon, I wouldn't have worn these shoes."

"Am I late?" Becky asked innocently.

"Moxley has just been waiting on you for ages," Kitty replied before she saw the cuff of Judge's suit. "What is that?"

"When I came out of the dry cleaner's, I ran into this fellow and dropped the suit. I'm afraid the cuff dipped into a puddle. But I think once it dries, it won't hardly be noticed. If I can…" Becky stopped when she saw her mother's face. It was sad and full of disappointment.

"Your father wanted that suit for the funeral for Mr. Foxworthy," Kitty said as she took it from Becky.

"It is black, Mama. I don't think it will be noticed down at the cuff, and I'm sure Lucretia can…" Becky stopped when her mother's hand went up.

"It's always for someone else to fix," Kitty said just as Moxley pulled up to the curb.

Only Fanny spoke on the way home. She was talking about something French. Kitty didn't reply, and Becky certainly didn't. Moxley sat uncomfortably in the driver's seat, keeping his eyes on the road.

Once they were back on the tobacco plantation, Becky was the last to get out of the car.

"You all right, Miss Becky?" Moxley asked.

"Moxley, did you ever have a time where everything you try to do right just turns out wrong?" Becky sighed.

"Yes, ma'am." He smiled kindly and nodded.

"What did you do to get things right again?" Becky asked.

"I waited out the storm. Trials don't last forever any more than those good times do."

"I guess you are right. Thanks, Moxley."

"Yes, ma'am," he said as he took some packages out of the rumble seat and carried them into the house.

Becky had the feeling if she apologized again to her mother, she'd just end up feeling even worse. Instead, she quietly went upstairs, closed herself up in her room, and took out her sketchbook and pencil. She drew Mrs. Hindergast and Mrs. Brower having a row in the middle of the sidewalk. It was one of her better pictures. But even as she sketched, the words Mrs. Hindergast had said or didn't say about Becky's life and behavior wouldn't leave her. Something was changing in her life, and she had a dark feeling that it wasn't for the better.

CHAPTER NINE

*I*t was the second day in a row that Becky heard her parents on the brink of an argument when she woke up and came downstairs. It nearly broke her heart.

"You obviously don't know how to talk to her," she heard Judge say.

"I guess I don't. That has always been your specialty. And she doesn't seem to be listening to you, either," Kitty replied.

Becky put her hand to her heart. This obviously had to do with the dry cleaning she had ruined and being late meeting Mama and Fanny in front of the bank. Add onto this great train of offenses missing the Jolly Corks show featuring her father, and Becky felt like a real heel.

"I don't have time for this, Kitty. You either fix it or don't. But I'm going to do what I said I was going to do," Judge said. "I won't be home until late."

Kitty didn't reply. Before Judge could see her, Becky ducked behind the stairs and out of sight. Her father smelled of cologne again, and he was snappily dressed, like he was going on a date. Was he? Was Becky's behavior pushing her parents apart?

Just as she came out from behind the stairs, she heard Kitty's footsteps coming in her direction. Her mother saw her immediately.

"Good morning, Becky," she said in a tired voice.

"Morning, Mama. How did you sleep?" Becky asked, hoping to get her mother to open up and talk to her. She knew how to talk to Becky. What Judge had said wasn't true. But she didn't want Kitty to know she had been eavesdropping. So she smiled and waited.

"Fine, dear," she replied.

"Is there anything I can help you with today? Any errands to run or chores around the house?" Becky asked.

"Why? What do you want now?" Kitty's voice was tired, and she wasn't at all like her usual self.

"I don't want anything, Mama. I'm just offering to help."

Kitty looked at her daughter suspiciously before shrugging. "I don't think I need anything, honey. Just go on to your cemetery or your fortune-teller friend or wherever it is you like to go," Kitty said. Then she smiled wearily before heading into the kitchen to speak to Lucretia about dinner that evening.

Becky turned and went back upstairs to Fanny's room. The door was closed. She pressed her ear against the cold wood and heard nothing inside, so she knocked. Still, there was no answer even after Becky opened the door.

"Fanny?" she called. "Fanny. Wake up."

"Who, what now?" Fanny rolled over and pushed her satin sleeping mask up over her eyes. "Good grief, Becky. What time is it?"

"It's after seven. I need to talk to you." Becky walked in and shut the door behind her. Without waiting for an invitation, she sat down on the corner of Fanny's bed.

"What is it?" Fanny asked as she scooted up in her bed and yanked her blankets up to her chin in a sudden display of modesty.

"Have you notice Mama and Daddy acting differently?" Becky asked.

"Different how?" Fanny said with a yawn.

"Does it seem to you that they're at odd ends?" Becky leaned forward.

"I haven't noticed them acting differently," Fanny replied.

"They've been snapping at each other for the past couple of mornings. That isn't like them. And they haven't yet forgiven me for missing Daddy's performance. Yet Mama has given me permission to go out without any lecture on behaving like a lady. It's like they've been replaced by two people who look and sound exactly like Judge and Kitty but don't act anything like them. Daddy has been talking in whispers and going out with his hair combed and cologne on. You haven't noticed it?" Becky hoped Fanny would say something that would put her mind at ease. She should have known better.

"Oh, he's probably having an affair," Fanny said casually.

"What?" Becky nearly fell off the bed. Part of her wanted to hear the rest of what Fanny had to say, but part of her wanted to beat the tar out of her for even thinking such a thing. Her inner turmoil caused her to just sit rigidly still and do nothing.

"Don't get your feathers ruffled. In Paris, it is very common for a man your father's age to take on a mistress. It isn't anything to worry about." Fanny snuggled under the soft, warm down of her quilt. "Especially if he's informed Kitty. Which it sounds like he may already have."

"I'm sure I'm not the only one to remind you that we are not in Paris. We are in the United States of America, and here in Savannah, only the lowliest of dogs would do such a thing," Becky hissed. "You'd better put a muzzle on it and never breathe a word of this scandal in mixed company."

"Rebecca, if that isn't what's got your parents in a bit of a tiff, then I'd have to say it might be you." Fanny blinked as she looked at Becky.

"If this is still about the Jolly Corks Minstrel show and missing Daddy's performance, I don't know how many times or ways I can say I'm sorry. If I have to hear one more word about it, I'm going to scream," Becky replied as she got up from the bed and paced to the other end of the room. When she turned around, Fanny was standing on her bed and looking down at her.

"You only think of yourself. Just drinking and dancing and your own affairs matter to you. Your parents know you don't really care about them, and it's driving them apart," Fanny said as if she were reciting a poem.

Becky stared up at her with her mouth hanging

open. She looked down at her bare feet against the hardwood floor then looked back up to find Fanny sitting in her bed, staring.

"Rebecca, what are you staring at?" Fanny asked.

"You...I...you were..." Becky rubbed her eyes. "Weren't you just standing on your bed?"

"Standing on my bed? Now why would I be doing such a fool thing as that?" Fanny scoffed. "Your mama is right. You live in your own world."

"Mama said that? When?" Becky asked nervously as she looked around the room for anything else that might be out of place.

"When *hasn't* she said it? Ever since I got here, she's said it," Fanny said while crinkling her nose.

"What should I do?" Becky went back to the edge of the bed and looked it over. There was no indentation from Fanny's feet in the thick comforter to indicate Fanny had climbed out of the covers.

"How should I know? You and I were raised in two completely different ways. I wouldn't know where to begin," Fanny replied as she patted the blond finger curls that had been pinned in place to make it through the night.

Becky couldn't take any more. She left Fanny's room feeling worse than she had when she went in. What bothered her most about what Fanny had said was that part of it might be true. Becky couldn't bear to think that her father would be stepping out on her mother. But the thought had crossed her mind, even if she didn't want to admit it. And a man did that when he wasn't happy at home. Perhaps Judge felt his responsibilities were becoming too much. Or maybe he was feeling unappreciated. That would be Becky's fault. She took her father for granted, always thinking she could do what she wanted and he'd always stick up for her.

That would explain the conversation she had heard this morning between her mother and father. Fanny was right. Becky had to have something to do with their bickering. Suddenly, sneaking around after No-cent and the conversation with Mr. Dover didn't seem so important.

CHAPTER TEN

That afternoon was hot. Becky had spent most of the day under the shade of a willow tree, sketching in the Old Brick Cemetery that butted against her family's property. The place had always brought her a sense of peace. Becky communicated with restless spirits there. They'd tell her about their families or the war or even the loves they were waiting to see again. But no one was very talkative today. Even Becky's usual visitors, those souls that recognized her, seemed to be too busy to pay her any mind. Maybe they didn't know she'd arrived. Or maybe they, like her parents, were tired of her shenanigans.

As Becky roamed along the weed-infested cobblestone path that snaked its way through the grounds, under the protection of the majestic trees that continued to grow and blossom every year without the help of a groundskeeper, her heart was heavy.

She contemplated becoming a member of the ladies' auxiliary like Kerry Merriweather in order to make her mother happy. But Becky knew she would be miserable. That just wasn't her.

But isn't that your problem, Rebecca? You're always thinking of what makes you happy and not caring what will make anyone else happy.

Becky heard these words outside her head and saw Mr. Wilcox standing off in the distance. He was one of her favorite friends from the ghostly realm. He'd spun her yarns about his family, so much so that she was sure she'd know them if she ever ran into them.

"But Mr. Wilcox, how can I make other people happy if I'm not happy?" Becky asked and quickened her pace to catch up with him, only to have him disappear before she reached him. He'd never done that before. Had he even been there to begin with? Maybe those words really had come from herself.

"Or maybe you've been out of doors for too long," Becky muttered. She wasn't hungry or thirsty. But the idea of a nap in her room, with all of her treasures that she'd collected over the years carefully placed around her, sounded like just the ticket. She headed back home and climbed the trellis and slipped into her room without anyone noticing.

Her room was her sanctuary. But this afternoon, as she stood in the middle of the room and looked around, she felt uneasy. Suddenly, the ticket stubs from the movies she'd seen were nothing more than clutter. She'd kept dance cards from Willie's New Year's Eve party. And there was a ball of string from balloons she'd bought hanging like colored vines over the side of her dresser. There were loads of feathers and multi-colored stones that she'd collected on her walks. There were Cracker Jack toys that she'd hung onto for years. What was she doing keeping all these silly things? Sure, they were fun and colorful, and there were some lovely memories attached to them, but where was the room for new memories and new adventures?

With a sudden burst of energy, Becky collected the memories and tucked them into the deepest corner of her hope chest. When she looked around her room, she felt as if she could breathe again. The clutter was gone not just from her dresser and vanity but from inside her head. She didn't have any idea what she was going to do about her parents. But at least now she could think. And she thought she was ready for a nap.

When Becky woke up, the sun was setting. No one had woken her up for supper. She was glad. She'd didn't have much of an appetite. But the warm night air was the perfect invitation to get out into the world.

The chance that Teddy was staying home was nonexistent. After washing her face and putting on a pretty dress and her most comfortable dancing shoes, Becky decided what she needed was a night out. Just as she swung her leg over the windowsill to make a clean getaway, Fanny barged in.

"Where are you going?" she asked, her hair already done up and her purse in her hand.

"Teddy's. Why?" Becky asked even though she already knew the answer.

"And you weren't going to tell anyone where you are going?" Fanny put her hand on her hip and blinked.

"No one seems to have any desire to talk to me. Isn't that right?" Becky asked, her thighs starting to ache from holding such an awkward position in the window.

"My, how you do go on. Well, you would have

made the trip to Teddy's for nothing. He's already got plans this evening." Fanny smiled.

"What do you know about it?" Becky asked as she climbed back into her room.

"While you were sawing logs, he stopped by. Seems everyone is going to Willie's tonight. He'll be here in a jiffy to pick me up," Fanny said before smoothing the front of her dress.

"You mean, to pick *us* up." Becky smiled and walked across her room and squeezed out the door past Fanny.

"That is the epitome of rude for someone to just invite themselves on a date," Fanny grumbled as she followed Becky downstairs.

"You aren't on a date with Teddy. Teddy and Martha have been together almost as long as I've known Teddy. Get any ideas about sinking your claws into him out of your head," Becky said as she stepped out the front screen door onto the porch.

Fanny had been right. Down the long dirt drive, she saw two familiar headlights.

"Oh, I would never think such a thing. But I can't account for what Teddy is thinking," Fanny said as she sashayed to the edge of the porch.

Becky rolled her eyes.

As soon as Teddy pulled up, he hopped out of the

car and gave her a big wink and howdy-do. "I knew I'd be seeing you tonight. Are you ready to trip the light fantastic?" Teddy asked, holding the car door open for Becky.

"Am I ever," Becky replied and gave Teddy a peck on the cheek. "You're looking mighty dapper tonight. Any special reason? And is that a new cologne I smell?"

"What's with the Edison act? Can't a gent get dolled up for his favorite ladies?" Teddy smirked as he shut the car door once Fanny had climbed in.

"Will Martha be meeting us?" Becky asked just to put a stop to Fanny's crazy ideas.

"Is the pope Catholic?" Teddy replied.

Becky lifted her chin as she looked straight ahead out the windshield. Fanny did the same. After some of the ice melted, Teddy started to chat again.

"Have you heard what's been going on at the fair?" Teddy asked. "I would have thought that after the turn at the pie tasting, the whole affair would have been behind the eight ball. Turns out Savannah is full of rubberneckers wanting to see where the whole thing took place. They've had so many people show up that there has been a line to get in almost every night."

"That's what I call morbid curiosity," Fanny replied.

"And that's not all. My father heard from his brothers in the Elks Club that everyone who submitted a pie is under suspicion. They all had some kind of bone to pick with Clem Foxworthy," Teddy said.

"How many people entered a pie in the contest?" Becky asked.

"Altogether, there were seven. And I heard one of the ladies had a rather special relationship with Foxworthy," Teddy added.

"Who was that?" Becky asked.

"Oh, what does it matter?" Fanny interrupted. "When I was in Paris, the men freely spoke of their mistresses."

"In front of their wives? That would get a guy bumped off over here. I always thought those guys had a few screws loose," Teddy said, and Becky was glad for it.

"Well, not in front of their wives, but it was common knowledge who had a mistress and who didn't. Grammy Louise always said you could tell who was a big shot and who was on the nut by the company they kept. You were a big shot in Paris if you had a mistress." Again, Fanny smoothed out her skirt.

"I don't know, Beck. Maybe I should head off to Paris. What do you think?" Teddy teased, making Fanny laugh.

"I think you might want to check with Martha first." Becky nudged him in the ribs as they pulled into the parking lot.

Within minutes, Becky had found Martha, who had a ciggy lit and ready for her as well as a champagne cocktail.

"You haven't been yourself, Beck. I'm worried about you," Martha said.

"You are a doll, Martha. There's been some beef at home with my parents. I love them so, Martha. I do. I just don't know how to be what they want me to be," Becky replied, shouting in Martha's ear over the music.

"What kind of high pillow do they want you to be?" Martha asked.

Becky jerked her chin toward Fanny, who had already found a spot at the bar and had one gent offering to light her cigarette while another was ordering her a drink, on the house.

"No. Do they know what a maroon she is?" Martha asked.

"Of course they don't. She's the bee's knees," Becky replied.

"I've known Aunt Kitty and Uncle Judge almost as long as you have, Beck. I don't think they want you to be like her. I think they are happy with you being you. I know I wouldn't want you any other way," Martha gushed as she held up her glass of champagne to Becky.

Without hesitating, Becky raised her glass, and they toasted one another before heading out onto the dance floor.

"Martha, are you ever worried about Teddy stepping out on you?" Becky asked.

"Why? Should I be?" Martha asked before taking another sip of her cocktail.

"No. I was just wondering if the worry ever crossed your mind," Becky replied.

"I'd be heartbroken, yes. But it's a big world out there. And don't tell Teddy, but I've always thought a beautiful sight was a man in a uniform." Martha giggled. Then Becky giggled. And before long, she'd forgotten her troubles and was having a swell time.

She'd kept her eyes open, hoping maybe Adam White would make an appearance. She hadn't seen him since the night he'd left her, promising to come back and then never returning. She'd felt a twinge of guilt that she'd barely given him a second thought, but there were too many distractions at home. Only now was she starting to feel like herself again and to see things a little more clearly. It was amazing what three champagne cocktails could do for a girl.

Becky danced and danced. She and Martha sang "I'm Forever Blowing Bubbles" and "Oh, What a Pal Was Mary" as they were played by the small band tucked into the corner to make room for everyone on the dance floor.

Only after several more songs did the conversation turn serious. Fanny returned to the table with a big palooka who wore a sharp suit and a gold pinky ring. He claimed to know for a fact that there was a girl involved in the murder of the Elks Club member and not just one but two other Elks who were fighting over her.

"How do you know this?" Becky asked.

"I got my connections," he replied with a smirk.

"Oh yes, I've heard of those fellows with their hands in the deep pockets of the Elks Club members. Trying to horn in on the fez market. Capone's Chicago ain't seen nothing till the Savannah Elks Syndicate makes the scene," Becky teased.

"Pay no attention to my cousin, Sean. She's a little rough around the edges," Fanny said.

"I can see that," Sean replied.

Becky rolled her eyes. "Sean? You obviously aren't from around these parts, or you'd know that half the people in this joint are related to someone who is a member of the Elks. Cracking wise about them might get you a sock in the puss."

"Oh, Becky. Settle down. Sean was only making conversation," Fanny interrupted.

"And so am I," Becky replied and smiled at Sean, who was looking her up and down.

"For such a little thing, you got a lot of spunk. I should have known by that red hair. Redheads are nothing but trouble. And I like trouble," Sean said with a wink.

"You don't want her kind of trouble," Fanny replied. "Why, did I tell you that because of her I got kidnapped?"

"What? I'd never let something like that happen to you," Sean replied, slipping his arm around Fanny's waist. She let him, but by the end of the night, Becky knew he'd be wondering where both his money and Fanny had gone.

As much as she tried to focus on having a good time, Becky couldn't help but take the words Sean had said to heart. Two Elks involved with another woman who was in the pie contest? It all sounded so intertwined and knotted together that Becky wanted to just toss it all aside. But something in her gut wouldn't let her quit. If she didn't snoop around a little further, her father could be in trouble.

That was all Becky needed to tell Martha she'd have to call it a night. Without wanting to rain on her friend's parade, and not wanting to explain anything to Fanny, Becky found Delilah and Zachary in the middle of a smooch session in his drop-top car.

"Did you two even make it inside?" Becky teased.

"Hi, Becky!" Delilah chirped. "Nice night, isn't it?"

"Hello, Becky." Zachary winced as if he'd just swallowed a spoonful of castor oil.

"Hey, you guys coming or going?" Becky asked.

"Going. Need a lift?" Delilah asked.

"That would be swell. I do appreciate it. Zach, can you keep away from Delilah's lips long enough to get me home?" Becky continued to tease.

"It'll be hard, but I'll try," he joked back.

On the way, the talk was all about the murder of Clem Foxworthy. Delilah and Zachary didn't have any more information than anyone else. The list of suspects was crazy enough. People speculated about who did what and why as if they were betting on the bangtails at Saratoga.

When she finally got home, Becky had Zachary drop her at the end of the driveway. The walk would give her a chance to wind down and think of what she was going to say to her parents if they were still up. But as she got closer to the house, once again, her best-laid plan was thwarted.

There was a strange car in the driveway, and it wasn't even parked all the way up to the door. It looked as if someone had driven up far enough to get to the porch but parked far enough back in the shadows so as not to be seen. Becky didn't recognize the car at all.

As she crept up to the porch, she heard a female voice speaking just over a whisper. "I can't do it anymore."

"You have to, Bernice," Judge said firmly. "Everything is going the way it is supposed to."

"I'm so tired of all this. You can't imagine how frustrating it all is."

It was Bernice Foxworthy. *The newly widowed Mrs. Foxworthy*, as Kitty had referred to her. She was in the Mackenzie house. Where was Kitty?

"Believe me. I do know," Judge replied. "But it will only be a matter of time. Kitty will understand once I explain everything to her."

CHAPTER ELEVEN

*B*ecky froze. She wanted to barge in and demand to know what was going on. But her body just wouldn't move.

"You'd better scram, Bernice. Kitty will be home any minute, and I don't think she'll understand. Not without my sitting her down and telling her everything," Judge said.

"If you say so, Judge. I don't know what I would have done if you weren't here," Bernice replied.

Becky was in such shock that she barely got out of sight when her father and Bernice Foxworthy stepped out on the porch. She clung to the trellis just a couple inches above the roof over the porch while her dress waved in the warm, lazy breeze.

"When will I see you again?" Bernice asked as she walked toward her car.

Becky didn't dare move. The slightest rustle of the ivy or scratch of her heel on the wood could give her away. When she heard her father's voice, the urge to turn her head was almost impossible to resist, but she did. Her heart was pounding as she listened to them talking softly to one another. After the way Judge had spoken to Kitty that morning before leaving the house, Becky wanted nothing more than to expose him. But she didn't. Instead, she held fast to the trellis, studying the leaves in front of her and trying not to move, shift, or burst into tears.

"I'll try and come by at the end of the week. We will have to see how things pan out," Judge soothed.

There was a silence before Becky heard the car door slam shut and the engine roar to life. Her hands and fingers had gone numb. Her legs were itching from the leaves tickling at them, and she knew she'd ruined another pair of stockings. Not to mention that her dress would probably have snags in it from the stiff vines. That would drive Kitty crazy. Becky thought of her mother instead of that awkward silence, which had been just long enough for a kiss between her father and this Bernice Foxworthy.

The car made a U-turn and sped out of sight as

Judge climbed the porch steps, went inside, and closed the front door. Becky pulled herself up the rest of the trellis and climbed through her bedroom window. Once inside, in the dark, she sat down on the edge of her bed and waited.

She didn't know what she was waiting for. Maybe she'd hoped her father would hear her and come to talk to her. Maybe she didn't want anyone to know she was there. Suddenly she was tired. Without worrying about washing her face, Becky kicked off her shoes and pulled off her ruined stockings then climbed into bed. As soon as her head hit the pillow, she began to cry. What was she going to do?

When morning came, she wasn't feeling any better. Even though she'd slept a deep, dreamless sleep, she felt terrible. Her body ached, and her head was full of cotton. The only problem with feeling like this today was that she didn't have the fun memory of painting the town red to go along with it. She had the awful memory of Judge and Bernice Foxworthy replaying itself in her head.

Before she could get up, there was a knock on her door. And before she could answer, her mother came in.

"Why, Becky, what are you still doing in bed?"

Kitty said, sounding much more like her old self. "Aren't you feeling well?"

"Oh, uhm…it was a rough night, I guess you could say," Becky replied. She absently threw her covers aside, revealing that she was still in her dress.

"Rebecca Madeline! You slept in your beautiful dress? I just bought you that dress not a month ago, and look at it. It's ruined." Kitty pointed. "And what is that? Did you stumble on your way home? It looks like you picked up half the county on the hem of your dress. Did you climb up the trellis again?"

"Yes, ma'am," Becky said, her eyes filling with tears.

"I honestly don't know what I'm going to do with you. Maybe your father can talk some sense into you, because you certainly don't listen to me." Kitty shook her head and looked around the room.

"Mama?" Becky sniffled.

"Oh, Becky, now don't cry. You are too big to start crying. Go wash your face and get ready for the day. I'll need your help, along with Fanny's, so please try to get along," Kitty said, paying no attention to Becky's emotional display.

"What do you need our help with?" Becky sniffed.

"It's my luncheon today, Becky. Goodness, have you already forgotten?" Kitty huffed.

"That's today?" Becky all but whimpered.

"Yes, it's today. Oh my. Let me guess. You've already made plans and won't be home to help. I should have known," Kitty snapped.

"No, Mama. I didn't realize it was today, but I'm at your service. Anything you want me to do I'll do. Did you want to pick out my dress for the day?" Becky pulled the tears back and forced a smile at her mother.

"Well, you certainly can't wear the dress you are in now." She huffed over to Becky's closet and opened the door.

Becky held her breath and watched as Kitty carefully examined every dress, going back and forth, until she finally picked one out. She whirled around and held up one of Becky's favorites. It was a pale-green drop-waist dress.

"That's lovely, Mama. I'll wear that." She smiled but got only a grunt in return.

"Would you mind waking up your cousin for me? I have no idea what time you girls got home, but from the looks of things, it was a wild night," Kitty said.

"I got home early. I didn't see you. Did you go

somewhere?" Becky waited for her mother to say something that would make all of last night seem normal.

Instead, Kitty patted her finger waves like she always did when she was nervous. "I went to visit Aunt Leona," Kitty said. "Now quick, honey. Get dressed. We have a lot to do."

Aunt Leona was Leona Bourdeaux, Martha's mother. And Martha hadn't said a peep about Kitty paying them a visit. It must have been rather late when Kitty decided to pop in. And that had made room for Bernice Foxworthy to slink over here and talk to Judge all by herself.

The last thing Becky wanted to do was pretend to enjoy the company of the ladies' auxiliary, but it was important to her mother. So Becky shook off her feelings of disappointment that she was stuck in the house all day with the hens of Savannah and marched across the hall to Fanny's room. She didn't bother to knock.

"Rise and shine!" Becky called, making Fanny sit bolt upright in bed, her sleeping mask pushed up over one squinting eye.

"What is the matter with you? Do you have no manners at all?" Fanny squawked.

"Mama's luncheon is today, and we need to help.

What time did you get in?" Becky asked. She walked over to the window and pulled the shade up, letting the bright morning sun come pounding in.

"Ugh! Rebecca! Shut that curtain!" Fanny groaned. "I don't know what time I came in. But after you left was when all the dust kicked up."

Becky whirled around. "What happened?"

"Oh, nothing, but Teddy decided he was going to pick a fight with a gent twice his size." Fanny scooted up on her pillow and pulled the covers up to her chin.

"Did someone put the make on Martha?" Becky asked with wide eyes.

"No. It wasn't over Martha. It was over you." Fanny sniffed and looked at Becky with a simp on her face.

"Me?"

Fanny nodded.

"Applesauce. You're daft. That Sean fellow slipped you a mickey, and you were seeing things," Becky harrumphed.

"Oh no. It was a big brouhaha. Sean had to get between them. I never knew Teddy had that kind of fight in him. He was ready to mop the floor with his face for you," Fanny continued.

"Well, what about? Who was he going to fight?" Becky asked.

"Adam White." Fanny's right eyebrow went up.

"Now I know you are off your rocker. Teddy and Adam are friends. They'd never throw punches at each other. You were drunk," Becky insisted. The whole scene didn't make any sense.

"Fine. Don't believe me. Martha will be here today. Ask her." Fanny yawned.

"Oh, I will," Becky said.

As if she didn't have enough to worry about with her own parents, now her best friend and her boyfriend were fighting. What was happening? Everything had gone crazy since Mr. Foxworthy was murdered. Was it all tied together? There was only one person who would know for sure, and Becky had been intentionally avoiding her. Madame Cecelia. She'd be honest and tell Becky what was going on.

Now Becky couldn't wait for her mother's luncheon to start. She bustled around the kitchen with Lucretia and Daisy as they prepared the food. She helped set out plates and the fine crystal. There would be gallons of sweet tea and nothing stronger than that. Becky was disappointed and hoped Martha would bring her flask.

Once the house was decorated with fresh flowers, every speck of dust had been wiped away, and each mirror sparkled without a single streak or smudge, the ladies started to arrive.

Finally, Becky spied Martha and Aunt Leona walking up the drive from the end of a long line of automobiles. She dashed out the door and politely waved and smiled at everyone until she reached Martha and her mother.

"My, Becky, you sure are looking pretty," Aunt Leona said as she gave Becky a quick hug.

"Thank you, Aunt Leona. Mama is inside. I do believe she's got a glass of sweet tea waiting for you." Becky smiled as she linked her arm through Martha's and gave it a squeeze.

"I'll need something stronger than sweet tea to deal with this crowd," Aunt Leona replied. She lifted her chin, strolled elegantly to the house, and left the girls to talk.

"What happened last night?" Becky tugged Martha's arm.

"I wouldn't have believed it if I didn't see it with my own eyes. My Teddy went after your Mr. White like a bulldog after a piece of ham," Martha said.

"What for? I thought they were friends." Becky shook her head.

"Well, it all started when that fella No-Cent came strolling in like some butter and egg man." Becky's mouth went dry. "You know, that boozehound who owes money to every speakeasy in town. Well, he pulls out a head of cabbage, pays his tab, and is about to leave when Adam comes strolling in."

"This isn't making any sense yet, Martha. Skip to the chase." Becky scratched her head.

"Well, No-cent has words with Adam just as Teddy joins them. Then Teddy and Adam start talking. The next thing I know, Teddy socks Adam right in the kisser. Then Adam grabs Teddy around the collar and is about to do a tap dance on his face when Fanny's big palooka steps in and spreads them out."

"Did Teddy say why he did such a thing? Was he lit?" Becky asked, hoping that it was a result of too much hooch.

"He didn't say a word to me. After that, he wasn't in the mood to swing, and I wasn't either. Fanny left poor Sean hanging by a thread, as usual, and we scrammed." Martha looked at Becky sadly.

"What happened to No-Cent?" Becky wasn't sure why she asked what had happened to the old rummy. The words just sort of fell out because she couldn't think of anything else to say.

"He slipped out during all the shenanigans. Didn't even stay for a drink. That in itself is a head-scratcher," Martha said, to which Becky nodded in agreement.

But what really bothered Becky was that her father had told No-Cent to leave town. She'd heard him herself. What was he doing still in Savannah with a roll of money and the notion to start an argument with Adam, who was at least ten years younger than him and six inches taller?

"Well, we'll just have to cheese it until we can talk to Teddy tonight. Martha, you got any giggle juice with you? Mama's running a desert in there." Becky sighed.

"Did you think I'd come to this shindig without any? You know me better than that, Miss Rebecca Madeline Mackenzie," Martha replied while pulling up her skirt to snag the flask from her garter.

They each took a sip then headed inside, where the ladies' auxiliary had already convened. The ladies were seated around the dining room table, in the adjoining sitting room, and in a couple of extra chairs pulled from Becky's and Fanny's rooms.

It was obvious from their choice in seats that Mrs. Hindergast and Mrs. Brower had yet to set their differences aside. Mrs. Brower was perched at the farthest end of the dining room table, with a gaggle of ladies she regularly socialized with sitting around her like wasps around a nest. Mrs. Hindergast was at the opposite end of the table, slightly to the right and out of Mrs. Brower's direct view. She also had a team around her.

Finally, Kitty came in with a fresh pitcher of sweet tea. Behind her was Lucretia, carrying the last tray of potato salad to be placed on the table before everyone would help themselves.

CHAPTER TWELVE

*A*s plates were filled and tea was poured, Becky stood back in the shadows, thinking about everything Fanny and Martha had said to her. No-cent had gone back on his promise to Daddy and stayed in town. Why would he do that unless it was part of some shakedown? But when the conversation turned to Clem Foxworthy's murder, Becky was all ears.

"It certainly has the Elks in a dither. Why, half of them are tripping over themselves trying to comfort Bernice Foxworthy in her time of need. The other half are trying to comfort each other now that their drinking buddy is gone," Mrs. Merriweather said then looked in Becky's direction.

Becky looked behind her to see who she was

glaring at only to realize it was her. All she could do was shrug, which made Mrs. Merriweather roll her eyes and look away.

"The man was poisoned. We should show a little respect," Mrs. Brower snapped. "He may not have been a good man in our eyes, but Bernice stayed with him."

"Well, what was that poor thing going to do? She didn't have anywhere to go," Mrs. Ross asked before taking a big bite of three-bean-salad.

"Everyone knew he had a girl on the side. For heaven's sake, she entered the pie contest too. He probably told her to and promised her the blue ribbon," Mrs. Hindergast replied as her cheeks got red with anger.

"She'd say that about anyone who got the blue ribbon besides her," Mrs. Brower whispered...loudly enough for everyone to hear.

"What was that, Caroline?" Mrs. Hindergast called out.

"Nothing, Tilly. Just making an observation," Mrs. Brower smirked.

"Don't think I didn't tell the police my suspicions about you, Caroline Brower!"

"Go right ahead, Tilly. I've heard that criminals often return to the scene of the crime. Wasn't that you at the tent last night when the fair was closing up? When you didn't think anyone was still around?" Caroline snapped. "The police know all about that."

"Ladies, let's remember there were other people who submitted pies, and all of them had an issue with Clem Foxworthy. I don't think there is a one of us here who doesn't have some kind of poison in our own house," Kitty said. "That doesn't mean we slipped it into a pie knowing he was going to eat it."

"Well, the tomato he was rumored to be squeezing had no business entering a pie in the contest. What is her name? Lucille Clementine. It was a slap in the face to poor Bernice," Mrs. Ross said. "Especially since I'd heard Bernice didn't know anything about her."

"Who did you hear that from?" Mrs. Merriweather asked before taking a sip of tea.

"Bernice herself," Mrs. Ross replied.

"Clem Foxworthy was stepping out with Lucille Clementine?" Caroline looked at Tilly. "I heard she suddenly appeared in town because her last beau was fit with a Chicago overcoat."

"And did you see her pie? It looked like she'd never baked anything before in her life. Blueberries were dripping on the plate." Tilly looked at Caroline who shook her head in disgust. If there was one thing that could unite the two rivals, it was a young floozy infringing on their pie-baking territory.

"Don't forget that new woman who entered," Caroline replied.

"What new woman?" Mrs. Ross asked, offended that she had been left out of some tidbit of town gossip.

"Oh yes. Ms. Natalie Phine. She's here from Alabama. Bought the old colonial down on Peachtree Lane," Caroline replied.

"Does she have children?" Mrs. Ross asked.

"Nope. She bought that huge house all for herself. Rather showy if you ask me. I've also heard she's tried to insert herself among some of the other families in town and has been seen spending quite a bit of money at the department store. They know her on a first-name basis at Gimbels," Mrs. Merriweather added.

"They know all of us on a first-name basis at the department store," Kitty interrupted.

"Only after years of repeat business," Mrs. Merriweather replied defensively.

"She wouldn't have had anything to do with Clem Foxworthy's death. She's not even from here," Mrs. Ross said.

"Don't be so sure. She's had just about every door

closed on her. She is a stranger, after all, and has a questionable past. Not to mention there is a rumor that she leaves her shades open at night," Mrs. Brower added. "Perhaps she had some dealings with Clem too."

Half the room chuckled while the other half nodded and continued to speculate on this new woman in town. No children. No husband. It was as if the woman had green skin and a clubbed foot.

"Didn't Elizabeth Gilmore submit a pie too?" Mrs. Merriweather interrupted.

All of this talk about women with suspicious backgrounds and men with loose morals made Becky feel she couldn't breathe. Had any of them caught even a slight whiff of Bernice Foxworthy at the Mackenzie plantation, it would turn into the biggest scandal since Hooker's Brigade. The way they all talked without regard for what was true and what was a fabrication made her want to burst into tears.

"Bless her heart, Elizabeth submits a pie every year but just doesn't have the right recipe." Mrs. Hindergast looked at Mrs. Brower and got another nod of approval for her comment.

"Let's not forget Mr. Dover, who also submitted a pie. It was common knowledge that he and Clem were at odds, to say the least," Mrs. Ross added. "And what is a man doing submitting a pie to a pie-baking contest to begin with? It's peculiar to say the least."

"Mr. Dover bakes. That's his hobby." Becky had had enough. "He told me so when I went to see him the other day. He said Mr. Foxworthy had it out for him. I don't know if that is true, but it's what Mr. Dover said. I'm not guessing. I'm not speculating. I'm not spinning a yarn. That's what he told me. Did he poison Mr. Foxworthy? I don't know. But apparently I don't know much, because I thought the ladies' auxiliary was in place to offer some folks a leg up. That doesn't sound like what's going on here. What this sounds like is everyone beating their gums. I'm sorry, Mama. If you'll excuse me."

Becky had been almost invisible in the corner of the room. That wasn't like her at all. Normally, she'd be buzzing around, making small talk and looking at the clock every few minutes to see how much longer before she could blow. But not today. Martha wasn't the only one who noticed it. Nor was she the only one who followed Becky upstairs.

"Wow, Beck. Where did that come from?" Martha asked as she joined Becky in her bedroom. "Your mama is going to be in a lather."

Becky flopped onto her bed and buried her face

in the pillow. "I know," she shouted into her pillow, making it come out as just a muffled grunt. When she rolled over to face Martha, her eyes were red.

"Beck, what's the matter?"

"Martha, I don't even know where to start. If I told you something, would you promise not to breathe a word of it to anyone? Not even Teddy?"

Martha made a cross over her heart and nodded before taking a seat next to Becky on the bed. It was something they had done since they were young girls. Becky adored Martha and knew if there was anyone she could talk to, it was her. In a voice no louder than a whisper during a Sunday church service, Becky told Martha everything that had happened since the day Clem Foxworthy was killed up until her catching Judge with Bernice last night.

"So, do you think Judge had anything to do with Clem Foxworthy's murder?" Becky sniffled.

Martha took her friend's hands and held them. "I think that what we need to do is go and talk to every person who had a pie in that contest and cross them off the list. And to be quite honest, I'm not convinced that Tilly and Caroline are innocent. You see how they get when a newcomer tries to get in on the action. I can't believe we are talking about pies.

But those two biddies would go to some lengths for another blue ribbon."

"You know your onions, Martha," Becky said.

"Last time I checked, you were running on all six yourself," Martha replied just as there was a knock on the door.

"Uh-oh." Becky wiped her eyes. "Come in."

Kitty appeared in the door. Becky felt her heart drop to the pit of her stomach.

"I'll go mind my potatoes," Martha said as she slid off the bed.

"No, Martha. You don't have to leave. Rebecca…" Kitty walked in and closed the door behind her. "I'm very proud of you for what you did just now. I swear, you surprise me at every turn."

"I surprise you?" Becky blinked.

"Yes, honey, you do," Kitty replied with a weak smile.

"Mama, are you all right? Is something bothering you?" Becky looked at her mother and saw she had a heavy weight on her shoulders. It wasn't the normal stress of having a daughter as different as Becky. It was something else.

"I have…no. Everything is fine. It's just these hot days get too me. I'll be thankful when September rolls around." Kitty forced a smile.

"Aunt Kitty, if you don't need us, would it be all right if I took Becky out with me for a spell?" Martha suddenly piped up.

Kitty folded her arms over her chest, and Becky was sure that a lecture was going to follow. "On one condition. You take Fanny along with you."

It was worse than a lecture.

"Of course Fanny can come along. The more the merrier. Come on, Beck. Let's grab your cousin and blow this pop stand. Thanks, Aunt Kitty," Martha said. She grabbed Becky by the hand like she'd done so many times over their years as friends and pulled her off the bed.

Kitty smiled. "You know, you two look just like you did when you were little girls and I'd find you up here playing dress-up. Except your hair was in pigtails, and Becky was always carrying on some conversation with herself in the corner of the room or out the window."

Becky had never told her mother that she could talk to spirits. Or that spirits talked back to her. Instead, she had let her mother think that she was nothing more than a creative little girl who had a vivid imagination. Martha knew and promised to take it to the grave with her, and she'd find Becky and continue being friends even in the afterlife.

CHAPTER THIRTEEN

"**I** don't know why you two wanted to leave Aunt Kitty's luncheon. I was finding the discussion lively and very enlightening," Fanny said as they hurried out of the Mackenzie house and to Martha's family car.

"One thing you need to remember about that group, Fanny. If they'll talk like that in front of you, you can bet they'll talk like that about you," Martha said as she got behind the wheel. Before she put the car in gear, she pulled her flask from her garter again and handed it to Becky.

"That's what was missing from Mama's luncheon. I swear, someday I'm going to spike that sweet tea and watch those women have the time of their life. I'll bet Mrs. Brower and Mrs. Hindergast would be hugging and crying like old war dogs if they had just a sip of juice," Becky said before taking a shot and passing the flask to Fanny.

"That's one thing they do not omit at any occasion in Paris. You have wine, brandy, champagne at everything from a baptism to a funeral," Fanny said before she took a dainty sip.

"We have alcohol at funerals. Remember when Carmine O'Shawnessey's great grandmother died?" Becky elbowed Martha, who laughed, nodding. "That entire three flat glowed in the dark everyone was so lit. I think the police were called at least twice, and the O'Shawnessey brothers, who were in their late forties, spilled out into the street, fighting with one another. And their women used language to make a sailor blush while cheering them on!" Becky doubled over as she laughed.

"Where are we going?" Fanny finally asked.

"To the old colonial house on Peachtree Lane," Martha said.

"What? Why?" Fanny sat in the middle of the back seat, her arms stretched across the seat top.

"To talk to Ms. Natalie Phine," Martha said.

Becky took a deep breath and felt better than she had in days. "If we're going to get to the bottom of this whole thing, someone needs to set the record straight."

"I don't know if this is a good idea," Fanny said.

"Of course it is. Just don't eat any pie if she offers you some," Becky teased.

With Martha at the wheel, they made it to Peachtree Lane in no time. The white colonial house stood by itself at the end of the street on a hill. There were men in overalls with paint smudges all over them climbing ladders and strolling across the grounds when Martha pulled up. The dirt driveway was lined with purple wildflowers, and tall broad-leafed evergreens stood on all sides. Becky noticed the painters were painting the black shutters a beautiful deep red. What a statement that was going to make to the biddies in town. She was afraid she was going to like Natalie Phine.

"Fanny, ask those fellows if the lady of the house is at home," Martha instructed.

"What? Why me?" Fanny grumbled.

"Because in that dress, they'll tell you. Heck, they'll probably tell you where the gold is buried and the combination to the safe," Martha snapped back while rolling her eyes.

It was just the kind of compliment that Fanny responded to. She got out of the car, and all work came to a halt to watch her walk up the dirt road. She spoke to a huge fellow who made her palooka, Sean, look like a pipsqueak.

Within seconds, Fanny waved to Becky and Martha, who hurried up the path to the front door.

"I know what the topic of their next bull session will be," Martha said as Fanny smiled at just about every gent who made a point to walk past. That was all of them.

"You're full of hot air." Fanny waved her hand as if she was shooing a fly.

Becky knocked on the door then looked at Martha. "What are we going to say?"

Just then, the door opened. A redheaded woman in a cream-colored dress with layers of black pearls around her neck answered the door. Unlike Mrs. Hindergast's plump figure, Ms. Natalie Phine's looked as if she'd swallowed a giant hourglass. Her hips were almost as wide as the front door, and when she smiled, she had two deep dimples in her cheeks.

"Yes?" Her voice sounded like slow jazz music on a hot night.

"Mrs. Phine?" Becky asked, hoping that she'd be able to come up with something to explain why she and her friends were standing on her stoop.

"The one and only. Can I help you ladies?" Her right eyebrow shot up suspiciously but the grin never left her lips.

Becky couldn't help it. She instantly liked the woman. After blurting out an awkward introduction, Becky took a deep breath and spilled the beans.

"We wanted to ask you about...the pie you entered in the pie-baking contest at the fair." Becky waited for her response.

"Oh, well, I think that might require a bit more time. Why don't you gals come in," Natalie said as she took a step back, allowing the girls inside.

"You have a lovely home, Ms. Phine," Fanny said. "I just love your bookcases. Books really are very decorative, don't you think?"

"Please, call me Nat. And you'd be surprised how good books are to read as well, darlin'. Now, what is it y'all want to know about my famous blueberry pie?" She waved them down the hall. The floor was covered with a red Oriental rug that muffled their footsteps across the hardwood.

Every inch of Nat's foyer was covered with paintings of strange yet beautiful images of gladiators, monks, flowers, and landscapes. One entire wall was filled with old books with exotic titles like *The Italian Romantic* and *Yoslav's Garden*. There were maps of Europe and Asia in elegant frames. The knickknacks perched alongside the books were nothing like the vases and children in lederhosen that Kitty had scattered about. They were elegant angels, strange animals, and odd things Becky had never seen the likes of. In the sitting room, there was a chaise lounge in front of an easel with a small table covered in paints. None of them could see the image on the canvas, as it was facing the other wall.

"Have you read all those books?" Martha asked.

"Most of them. I've got a few in the big library that I haven't dove into yet." She squinted her heavily lined eyes then ran her hand through the beads around her neck.

"The big library?" Becky gasped.

Nat's blue eyes snapped in Becky's direction. "Why, sure. Good ideas come from the strangest places. But I prefer not to waste a lot of time and look for them in books." Nat chuckled. "So, this visit is about the pie?" She sat down on the chaise lounge like a cat stretching in the sun and looked at Becky before motioning for her to take a seat in the love seat across from her.

"Well, I'm sure you heard what happened at the fair," Martha said as she took a seat on the edge of an elegantly carved armchair. Fanny sat down next to Becky in the love seat.

"Oh yes. Poor Clem. I heard he was poisoned," Nat said.

"So you knew him?" Becky asked.

"Oh, honey. Guys like Clem come a dime a dozen. I've met at least six just like him over the past year." She waved her hand, showing off bright-red nails that matched her lipstick.

"Did you know he was married?" Becky continued.

"Of course I did," Nat replied.

"And you went out with him anyways?" It was Martha's turn to gasp.

"What? Hold your horses. I just wanted to get to know the people of this fine town and thought that if I entered the pie-baking contest and a couple folks tasted my wonderful blueberry pie, I might make a few friends. Seems like people in Savannah ain't the most hospitable to strangers," Nat replied. "Aside from Clem and that Bruno out painting my shutters, I haven't had an invitation anywhere from anyone."

"Do you suspect anyone in the contest who might have slipped the poison into their pie to poison him?" Martha asked.

"Honey, I don't know anyone well enough to send them to the hoosegow. But a man who cheats on his wife should be more afraid of the woman lying next to him in bed than anyone else. Whether that woman is his wife or the mistress," Nat replied with a chuckle.

Those words sent a shiver up Becky's spine. Could it have been Bernice who had done this to Clem? And if she did, what would she do to Judge if he turned her away?

"I'm putting my money on Mr. Dover. Any man who enters a baking contest has to be a bit jingle-brained," Martha said.

"Oh, I wouldn't say that. I've known some men who were geniuses in the kitchen. If it weren't for them, I wouldn't have this here figure of mine!" Nat laughed loudly and everything jiggled. Her laugh was genuine and came from deep inside, making Becky laugh without even realizing it.

"So, I guess Mrs. Hindergast and Mrs. Brower were wrong about you. They didn't care too much if you went to the hoosegow. But you didn't put poison in your blueberry pie?" Becky asked, regretting each word as it left her mouth. Could she sound more stupid?

"That would be a very bad way of making

friends, don't you think?" Nat winked at Becky. "Are you an artist?"

"I am," Becky replied. "How did you know?"

"She's a great artist. I don't know how she does it, but she can draw people just the way they look. Even when they look grumpy," Martha boasted.

"You have that lump on your finger from where the pencil presses against your skin. Only artists have such a defined callus," Nat replied. "When I was in Europe, I met quite a few artists."

"You went to Europe?" Fanny's ears perked up.

"Oh yes. Of course. London. Rome. Paris. Warsaw. Dub..." Nat stopped when she was interrupted.

"You were in Paris? Why, I've been to Paris too." Fanny scooted to the edge of the seat, prepared to dazzle Nat with her adventures in parties, social gatherings, and whatnot.

"I was not impressed. I'll take those Italian artists any day over the French. The food too. So much passion and machismo." Nat smiled. "I could tell you about my time in France. I was bored out of my gourd. But my time in Italy, well, I think you ladies might be too young."

Martha leaned forward and smoothed out her

skirt. "Please, do tell. This is much more interesting than who killed Clem Foxworthy."

"In fact, it was in Italy that I learned to bake blueberry pie. I know it isn't your typical Italian dessert, but the man who taught it to me added a few special ingredients that gave it a truly unique flavor. I would have won the blue ribbon had Clem not died." Nat shrugged. "You didn't really think I could do such a thing, did you? Even if you'd never met me. Who goes around poisoning strangers? No. If I have a beef with you, you can bet we'll go toe-to-toe."

Fanny pinched her lips at Nat then looked at Martha before she jerked her head toward the door. Martha shook her head before standing up to admire the books on the shelves and inch her way closer to the canvas on the easel.

"I'd hate to think of what would have happened to you if you had won the blue ribbon," Martha replied. "Mrs. Hindergast and Mrs. Brower have been competing in the pie contest for as long as I can remember, and they don't take too kindly to outsiders trying to horn in on what they consider their birthright: the blue ribbon. It's one thing to lose it to someone from town. Even that might get you ostracized. But it's another to have a total stranger outdo you."

"From the sound of it, maybe you girls should be talking to Mrs. Hindergast and Mrs. Brower. Has anyone dared approach them? I've met merchant marines who sounded more pleasant." Nat chuckled again.

"You've met merchant marines?" Becky asked. It wasn't as if she didn't know what those were. They were regular fellows on the ships that ran along the coast. But there was always something exotic about them, since they weren't actually military but had their life on the water. Everything Nat was saying fascinated Becky.

"Sure. Where do you think I got this oyster fruit from?" She held up a couple of strings of black pearls from around her neck. "Honey, there's a whole world out there."

"I've heard those men can be dangerous," Fanny said.

"No more dangerous than poor Clem, and you see what happened to him. And from the sound of it, you gals are of the mindset that a female laid him low. Am I right?" Nat asked.

"Uhm…yes," Becky said, feeling like a child at a dance for the big girls. Natalie Phine had a maturity about her that Becky wanted for herself. Here she was in this beautiful home—from what she could see, the rooms were filled with books, paintings, and lovelies of all sorts from all different places. It was the perfect complement to Madame Cecelia's small apartment, which was also stocked with interesting tapestries, spices, and trinkets.

"Ha! Well, you girls have been a breath of fresh air. At least you came to visit me directly. I walk down the street on my way to Gimbels, and I'm all but ignored. Sure, the salespeople are nice to me, but when they know you have money to throw around, everyone is nice to you." She laughed and slapped her knee. "And I'll say it again just for the record: I did not poison Clem. I don't even know the man's last name. All I know is he doesn't even have the decency to take off his handcuff when he's hot to trot. Some shebas go for that. Not me. I like my men like I like my tomes: interesting, well read, and able to stand on their own." She took a thick dark-green book with gold lettering from her coffee table and stood it on its end. It balanced perfectly. Even a good bump of the table wouldn't knock it down. "Sorry you came all the way out here for nothing."

"Well, thank you for inviting us into your lovely home," Martha said as she finally wandered to the canvas on the easel. The look on her face was enough to tell she had not expected what she saw.

"Now that y'all know the way, please come pay ol' Nat a visit again sometime. I bet we'd have a lot to chat about." She smiled before picking up her long black cigarette holder and inserting a fresh cigarette in the end.

"Do you really mean that?" Becky asked.

"Of course I do, honey," Nat replied kindly. "I always seem to fall in with the misfits in the towns I take up residence in. I hope that don't offend you none. I find it's made my life quite interesting."

"I can communicate with spirits," Becky blurted. "I've been able to do it as far back as I can remember."

"Well, now. That is a new one on me. But I sure would like to hear more about it when you've got the time. I've read many books on that topic. You'd be surprised at the number of people in history who have claimed the same gift. I'd love to pick your brain, if you don't mind," Nat said as she walked them to the door.

"That sounds ducky," Becky replied. Martha and Fanny hurried out the door, Fanny especially making a beeline to the car and paying very little attention to the catcalls and whistles.

"You have a good heart, Miss Becky," Nat said. "And that Martha gal is a good partner in crime to have alongside. But I must ask, where did you dig up that dumb Dora?"

"She's my cousin," Becky replied as if she was admitting to a case of lice.

"Leave it to blood relations to bring ants to the picnic." Nat shook her head and smiled.

"It was really nice meeting you, Nat." Becky turned and extended her hand.

Nat accepted her handshake firmly. "Come see me again. I'll bet we have a lot to talk about."

Nat stepped onto her front porch, and the men quickly forgot about Fanny and focused on the lady of the house.

"Hey, Nat. We finished with the front shutters. You want the back shutters painted too?" asked the same man Fanny had approached when the girls first arrived.

"No, Jake, I want just the front half of my house done. Of course, paint the back shutters too. And you better not let me catch you or your boys sleeping on the job." Nat winked with her hands on her curvy hips.

"No one's sleeping with you around, Nat," Jake joked.

"And when you're all done, I'll have a bucket of suds on that old jalopy waiting for you."

"You're the cat's pajamas, Nat," Jake replied. He turned and ordered his men to move the equipment around to the back of the house.

Becky waved to Nat one last time before Martha got the flivver turned around. Within seconds, they were jostling down the dirt road and back toward civilization.

"I can see why everyone was suspicious of Nat. She's beautiful and smart and looks like she knows a thing or two," Becky said. "I like her."

"Oh, you would fall for a ruse like that." Fanny huffed. "You like that strange Gypsy woman too. And I've heard some very strange rumors about her as well. Like when there is a full moon and where her family comes from."

"And this has nothing to do with Nat putting the kibosh on your stories of Paris?" Martha asked.

"Of course not. Not everyone can appreciate the Parisian lifestyle. Natalie obviously was not introduced to the finer families of Paris like I was," Fanny replied.

"Well, I don't care what you think. I like her."

"Did either of you get a look at the painting on the easel?" Martha asked with wide eyes. Becky and Fanny both shook their heads.

"Why?"

"It's Nat, stark naked from the waist up. All I could think was that had Mrs. Brower or Mrs. Hindergast caught a glimpse of that, they'd have kittens on the spot." Martha wailed with laughter.

"You know, I never spoke to Mrs. Brower about her blueberry pie. Do you think she could have done it?" Becky asked.

"I think that if Mrs. Brower thought she could get away with it, she'd poison someone else's pie," Martha said. "It's a sad state of affairs to think such things about the neighbors we've grown up with. But remember that time when that sweet old lady won the best spring garden contest?"

"Martha! I forgot all about that!" Becky gasped.

"What happened?" Fanny asked.

"You saw Mrs. Brower at the house. She's a thin rail of a woman. Looks like a baby bird with big peepers and scrawny legs. You wouldn't think she could harm a fly," Martha said.

"Yes," Fanny answered.

"Mrs. Tobin was about sixty years old when she entered the spring garden contest along with about a dozen other residents in town. The lady had a green thumb. There was no doubt about it. Everyone knew it. She could take a plant, brown, curled leaves with just a spot of green left on it, and not only revive it, but heck if the thing wouldn't grow and bloom like a canceled stamp at the USO."

Becky laughed and nodded. "It drove Mrs. Brower batty. And it's getting closer and closer to the day when the judges walk all over the town, admiring the gardens and giving them a score. Mrs. Brower is starting to panic."

"Panic? She was having a full-blown conniption fit. She had convinced herself that Mrs. Tobin was cheating somehow. Then she lost her marbles." Martha nodded. Her face became deadly serious as she focused on the road. "It was after a rainstorm. I remember because we took to the cellar that night for fear a twister might set down."

"I remember that too," Becky replied.

"Wouldn't you know, there were terrible winds and a whole lot of lightning. But no uprooted trees or fires from lightning. It was just a bad storm. When the sun came up, everyone was working on all cylinders, since nothing was out of the ordinary. Except for Mrs. Tobin's garden. It had been ripped up from the roots. Not a single flower was left in the dirt. It looked like a thousand moles and groundhogs had torn up her flowerbeds. And just the flowerbeds. Every tree and bush was still in place. It was just Mrs. Tobin's flowers."

Fanny gasped. "That woman who was in your house this afternoon did that?"

"There was a hitch. No one saw her do it. But when she came sashaying up to her cliques of kin, saying that it sure was a shame the storm set down right on Mrs. Tobin's lawn, everyone knew she'd done it." Becky shook her head.

"I'm shocked," Fanny said.

"So Mrs. Brower had to go out into this terrible storm and pull up each daisy, each rosebush, each gladiola, each tiger lily, everything with her own hands. And sure enough as I'm sitting here, I can recall my mother telling my father that Mrs. Brower's hands looked like they'd gone through a meat grinder," Becky said.

"And no one did anything?" Fanny asked.

"She said she fell into her own rosebush. There was no one there to witness that, either," Martha replied.

"I don't know. You two are trying to pull the wool over my eyes with some yarn about that woman. I don't believe it." Fanny shook her head.

"Believe it or don't. Just don't cross Mrs. Brower when she's trying to win another blue ribbon," Becky said.

She'd almost forgotten about that story, since so

many things had happened in her life since then. That had to have been almost six, maybe even seven years ago. Mrs. Brower hadn't had any serious competition in the beautiful garden contest since, now that Becky thought about it. And in the pie-baking contest, the only real competition was Mrs. Hindergast.

"Who won the pie contest last year?" Becky asked Martha.

"I do believe that Mrs. Hindergast has won the past couple of years," Martha replied.

"So Mrs. Brower certainly has a motive," Becky said.

"She does. But why would she poison her own pie?" Martha scoffed.

"Mrs. Hindergast told me that if Mrs. Brower had the chance, she'd slip a mickey in someone else's pie if she thought it would guarantee her a win. Maybe she didn't mean to put enough poison in to kill a man. Maybe she just wanted Mr. Foxworthy to get sick. Sick enough to disqualify Mrs. Hindergast from the competition," Becky said.

"I think you are both crazy. There isn't any proof of anything you are saying," Fanny interrupted. "Why, if I didn't know any better, I'd think you were just looking for ways to get revenge yourselves."

"Revenge for what?" Martha huffed.

"Well, maybe not you, Martha. But Becky here certainly hasn't been invited to any of the homes of the finer families in town," Fanny scoffed.

"Applesauce!" Becky snapped.

"As long as I've been here, all I've heard from the women in town is that you are peculiar and do things for attention without thinking of anyone else," Fanny replied.

"Becky is the most genuine person you'll ever meet. They should all be taking a lesson from her and not the other way around. Mark my words, Fanny. One day, you'll be bragging that Rebecca Madeline Mackenzie is your cousin," Martha retorted.

"Of course you'd say that. You're her friend," Fanny muttered under her breath.

"I'm warning you, sister! You'll be hoofing it back to the plantation if you don't pipe down." Martha gripped the steering wheel tightly until her knuckles were white.

Becky was only half listening to Fanny, as usual. There was no use arguing with her. No matter what Becky did, Fanny would find a way to ruin it. The truth was that Martha had struck a nerve by bringing up Mrs. Brower's past. And Nat had said something else that had stuck with Becky like the spiny cockleburs that always clung to the hems of her dresses. "If she had a beef with you, you can bet she'd go toe-to-toe." Becky was starting to feel that way herself.

CHAPTER FOURTEEN

hen Martha dropped Becky and Fanny off at the Mackenzie planta-tion, it was almost dinnertime. Fanny grumbled all the way into the house and up the stairs about how she should have stayed home with the ladies' auxil-iary instead of going out to Nat's. Becky saw all the dishes had been neatly washed and stacked on the dining room table in order to be put away later. She walked into the sitting room, peeked in the kitchen, and went round to the den without any sight of her mother.

"Mama?" Becky called.

She went upstairs to her parents' room and peeked inside. Kitty was sitting on the edge of the bed.

"Mama? Are you okay?" Becky asked after gently knocking on the door.

"Honey, I didn't hear you come in. Oh yes. I'm fine," Kitty replied even though Becky was sure she'd been crying.

"Did something happen after we left? Did the ladies give you a hard time about me? I'm sorry, Mama. I'll apologize to each and every one of them. If it will make things better, I'll…"

Kitty shook her head. "No. That won't be necessary. It was Mrs. Hindergast and Mrs. Brower who should be apologizing to everyone. Those two are like a couple of rabid dogs around one another," Kitty said, smirking. "Remind me never to invite them over at the same time again."

"Why did you invite them in the first place?" Becky asked.

"Because it's what's expected, Rebecca," Kitty said with a tired smile.

Becky didn't like the sound of that. But she didn't argue with her mother. Instead, she told her where she and Martha and Fanny had gone.

"You did what?" Kitty didn't shout, but it was obvious from her stare that she wasn't happy with her daughter going to the home of a strange woman with no ties to any of the families in town.

"She was lovely, Mama. She had books in her home from floor to ceiling. And she's been all over Europe and…"

"If you want to know about Europe, you could try talking to your cousin Fanny," Kitty urged softly.

"Are you off your rocker?" The words just slipped out, as they sometimes did.

"Becky?"

"I'm sorry again, Mama. But trying to get a true story about Paris out of Fanny is like trying to hug a porcupine. No matter how delicate you try to be, you're still going to get stuck," Becky replied with a chuckle. "Besides, Nat has been to other places besides Paris. I think you'd like her."

"I don't want to hear any more about it. When I let you girls leave the meeting, I thought you'd be going to do something constructive," Kitty said with a sigh.

"Making a new member of the community feel welcome isn't constructive? I'll remember that the next time you tell me to take Fanny along with me."

"You are just like your father." Kitty huffed as she pushed herself off the bed.

"Where is Daddy?"

"He's out. He won't be home until late," Kitty said flatly.

"He's been gone a lot lately," Becky said, hoping her mother might shed some light on the situation.

The words of Nat's that had struck such a chord seemed to fall flat as she looked at her mother. Becky had always seen Kitty as the perfect portrayal of a Southern lady. But lately, her mother looked lost and worn. And when Kitty didn't reply to her comment, Becky didn't push any further.

Becky didn't say another word. Instead, she quietly left her mother's room and went to her own, shutting the door tightly. As she looked around, she saw some more things she no longer wanted to keep: some old gloves that had long ago been stained on the fingers, a couple of books she'd read as a child. She threw open her closets and began sorting through her clothes.

As she went through her things, memories seemed to cling to every piece of clothing. Some of them were better than others. She had been wearing her black sleeveless dress the first time she'd entered a speakeasy. The time Teddy had had to literally carry her out of Willie's because she'd gotten her toes smashed by some corn-shredder she had been wearing her peach blouse. And then there was the first time she'd seen Adam White. She'd never forget that night. It was warm, and he was a tall drink of water at the opposite end of the joint, staring at her as if she'd just flashed him her knees.

It had been several days since she'd seen him, and suddenly, she felt terribly guilty. As she collected the clothes that she no longer wanted, despite memories she was sure she'd never forget, and put them aside to pack up later, she decided she was going to go out tonight and make up for some lost time.

Her father's absence weighed down the back of her mind like a pigtail pulled too tightly. But she couldn't battle every windmill at once. And a night out with her favorite fella was hardly a crime.

She looked through her closet and found a blue dress that still had the receipt pinned to it. There were no black pearls in Becky's jewelry box, but she had three strands of white ones and thought they would look just ducky. And in this dress, she wouldn't shimmy down the trellis. She'd walk out the front door.

When Teddy showed up in his flivver with the top down, Becky felt a second wind kick in. She did as she'd promised herself and went into the sitting room, where her mother was reading a book.

"Teddy's here. I'll be back later." She kissed her mother on the top of her head.

"All right, honey. Don't think that everyone isn't

going to be talking about you now that you went to that Natalie Phine's house and made a scene at my luncheon," Kitty hissed.

"What?" Becky shouted.

"What, what? I said don't be too late. Your father called and said he might need your help tomorrow on the plantation," Kitty replied.

"Oh, I'm sorry, Mama. I didn't hear you right. That's all." Becky shook her head. This was the third time she'd heard cruel and hurtful words from her family, and yet they acted as if they hadn't said them. Did they say them? Was she hallucinating? What was going on?

"Have fun. Say hello to Teddy, and tell Mr. White he shouldn't be such a stranger," Kitty replied before going back to her book.

Becky wondered if she'd heard that right. Adam had gone out of his way to make an impression on Becky's parents and assure them he wasn't the reincarnation of Abraham Lincoln just because his family came from the North. It had been a treacherous journey, but he'd done it. In no time, he'd won over Judge. Kitty was a somewhat tougher nut to crack, but he'd managed to soften her up a good bit.

When Becky walked out the front door, even Teddy was surprised.

"Uh-oh. What's wrong? Did Judge finally nail your window shut to keep you from escaping?" he teased.

"Very funny. No. I just thought it's about time I use the front door. I'm not a kid anymore," Becky replied.

"That you are not. Especially in that dress. I'm going to have to pick up a whip and a chair to keep the sharpshooters away."

"You won't have to. Do you know where Adam might be hiding out tonight?" Becky asked.

She and Adam had regular dates, but there were times like this when they just missed each other. She'd leave one joint and he'd be there ten minutes after they left. Sometimes he had to work late at the printing press or the gang wanted to go to a party on the other side of town. It was inevitable that they'd find each other. And it would be like dancing with him for the first time all over again.

"Uh, no. But we can go looking," Teddy said.

"What's this I hear about you trying to pick a fight with him?" Becky asked.

"That was just a little too much giggle juice, doll. Nothing for you to worry about," Teddy said quickly and gave her chin a light tap with his fist.

"Martha said it was one for the books. Did he say something to make you mad?" Becky continued.

"No," Teddy replied. "Like I said. I was lit, and he walked in. He just happened to catch me in a bad mood."

"In all the years I've known you, Teddy. I've never known you to be in a bad mood."

"How'd you manage to drop anchor and leave Fanny behind? Leave Fanny behind, did you hear that?" Teddy chuckled at his own joke, and that made Becky laugh.

"She didn't want to go out. We met that new woman in town who lives in that old colonial on Peachtree Lane," Becky boasted.

"I heard all about her from the bull session at the Elks Club. I was picking up my dad. The things they were saying about her made her sound like a voodoo priestess putting a spell on just about every gent in the joint." Teddy clicked his tongue. "If you catch my meaning."

"She's very glamorous. But the crazy thing is she's really smart and is a regular Charlie Chaplin with the laughs. Really, Teddy, she's just what this town needs to shake it up a little."

"Right, because the death of Foxworthy hasn't shaken things up enough. Did you know that Barlocceli's Bakery hasn't sold a single pie since the incident? Thank goodness he hasn't stopped making those canolini things." Teddy licked his lips.

"They are called cannoli. And what do you say we go back to the Elks Club tonight?" Becky said.

"I don't think there is anything going on there. And even if there was, my dear, you can't come in. It's for boys only." Teddy bounced his eyebrows.

"All the more reason I should go in when no one is around." Becky grinned and batted her lashes as she looked over her shoulder at him.

"What gives?"

"I think there might be something that got missed that might tip us off to what really happened to Foxworthy. He was quite a ladies' man from what I've heard, and…"

"I hate to break this to you, Becky, but a man stepping out on his wife isn't a crime. It don't cut the mustard, I know, but a fellow can't get tossed in the cooler for it. And he certainly can't be sentenced to death for it. I think we ought to go to a club and forget about all this. Tell me more about your new friend. She sounds like a dream," Teddy joked, but Becky wasn't smiling.

"Theodore Rockdale, after all the times I've practically carried you to your front stoop after you drank too much. And all the times I've walked home by myself, cutting through the dark, scary foliage that is between your house and mine just so you wouldn't have to exert yourself." Becky huffed.

"Don't do it, Rebecca Madeline!" Teddy scoffed.

"And to think if it weren't for me, you would never have met the love of your life, Martha Bourdeaux. And all I want is a lift to a place that isn't even out of the way. But that is just too much to ask." Becky shook her head.

The truth was that she wanted to see if there was anything about Foxworthy's life that might shine a light on who could have killed him, but more importantly, she was hoping something that might clear her father would pop up. There was nothing to point her in any other direction except that he was somehow involved. But she couldn't believe it. He just couldn't be, and she was willing to risk her skin to find out something, anything, that would erase the thoughts that her father was having an affair.

For a moment, she contemplated telling Teddy. He was as dear to her as a brother. But before she could, he spoke first.

"All right. I'll take you. But you've got ten minutes before I leave you there for the loudest, hottest juke joint in town," Teddy said.

"It's a deal." Becky clapped and smiled as Teddy pushed the flivver to go faster.

However, it didn't take long for Becky's plans to be derailed once again. As they approached the Elks Club, a paddy wagon was there already.

"Pull off here and hide," Becky said.

"What? Are you missing an oar? We should just turn around like we are lost and head out of here," Teddy said.

"I can't do that. But look, Teddy, I don't want you to get in trouble over me. You go on and make tracks. I'll catch up to you." She smiled at Teddy and nodded before she climbed quietly out of the car.

Teddy clicked his tongue and let out a deep sigh. "You always were the adventurer. I'll be under those boughs, and don't make me wait. Ten minutes, Becky. I mean it."

"Ten minutes," she whispered and took off into the shadows of the trees that surrounded the Elks Clubhouse.

As she crept closer, she could hear the police asking questions. A handful of members was milling about, all of them offering answers. The only question Becky actually heard was directed to someone she knew.

"Mr. Dover, you had a problem with Mr. Foxworthy?" the copper asked.

"Not really. We were different, but I'd say he was a fine fellow," Mr. Dover said with his hands in his pockets and his face looking uninterested.

That's a lie, Becky thought. Mr. Dover had had nothing nice to say about Clem Foxworthy when she'd stood in his kitchen.

Mr. Dover went on to say that he and Mr. Foxworthy were just getting to know each other and that he found him a pleasant fellow. Why was he telling the police one story when he'd spilled his guts to her in his own kitchen, saying the man was no good at all? Could it be that he had something more to do with it? Had she been duped?

All she could think was that as soon as the news hit the headlines that Mr. Dover was responsible for the gruesome death of Clem Foxworthy, Mrs. Merriweather, Mrs. Hindergast, and Mrs. Brower would be knocking on Kitty's door to point out how wrong her daughter was and how they all expected an apology for being so rudely addressed at the luncheon. Becky thought maybe she should learn to keep her mouth shut. Oh, it made her sick in her heart to think of her mother facing that group of shrews.

She crept closer. There was an open door at the side of the club, the same one her father had come out of the day he'd paid off No-Cent. Light shone from it. Without waiting, Becky bolted across the lawn and made it to the side of the building. She pressed her back against the cold stone and tried to calm her breath. She slipped inside the cracked door. A coatroom for staff led to a long hallway. She heard voices at the end of it and proceeded carefully. The light overhead was bright compared to the darkness she'd been used to outside. Within seconds, her eyes adjusted, and she inched her way closer to see several Elks standing in groups, all whispering and muttering to one another.

"Clem's been a pain in life and now he is in death," one man said.

"I blame Judge."

Becky's heart stopped as she peeked around the corner to get a look at who was speaking.

"If he didn't insist on doing the Jolly Corks show, he would have been the judge for the pie contest."

"He had his reasons for declining that task," another man said. "He's dealing with a lot right now, especially at home. I don't begrudge the man for trying to find a little peace."

Becky swallowed, but her mouth had gone dry.

What were they talking about? She wanted nothing more than to dash out there and grab that man by the collar. A good shake or two might get him to tell her what he meant when he said her father was having problems at home.

But she didn't dare. Instead, she slipped out of the hallway and hurried toward the lobby of the building, where the police were still asking the members questions.

"Clem was a good man. A little scratchy, but what man isn't like that at certain times?" another man said. Why were they all covering for him?

"The only man who I ever knew to have any beef with Clem was Judge Mackenzie. They'd had more than one altercation in front of everyone. I think there was something going on there that involved Mrs. Foxworthy that…" Mr. Dover stopped short.

"That isn't true!" Becky didn't know what she was doing. All she knew was that she couldn't stop. It was just like dealing with the old hens at her mama's luncheon. But she had been invited to that event. Here, she was a crasher.

The place became so quiet that all Becky could hear was her heart beating in her ears.

"Mr. Dover, you're lying!" Becky huffed. "You told me different the other day when you invited me into your home for pie. You said Mr. Foxworthy was an awful man. And in addition, you had a bottle of strychnine right on your kitchen shelf."

"Becky Mackenzie, what are you doing here?" It was the voice of Mr. Merriweather.

Becky swallowed hard as she looked at the man. "I'm not going to let Mr. Dover speak ill of my father when Daddy isn't even here to defend himself!" Becky shouted.

"Young lady, this is a private club. I don't care if you are Judge's daughter. You are trespassing on private property. In addition, you are displaying very unladylike qualities. I cannot allow this sort of disrespect to go unchallenged." The man speaking looked to be at least a hundred years old and as ornery as a barn owl.

"Now, let's just calm down," the copper said, holding his hands out with his fingers splayed. "Miss Mackenzie, I know your father. I believe he'd be mighty ashamed of you infringing on the clubhouse of these fine gentlemen."

Becky stared at the policeman with eyes wide with anger and fear. "If you know my daddy, then you know what Mr. Dover is saying is a lie. How can any of you just stand here and let him talk that way? My father has helped most of you out at one time or another. How can you let someone talk about him in such a way?"

"That's enough, Miss Mackenzie. Come with me," the policeman said as he led Becky out by the arm out.

"Officer, I'm afraid that it will be necessary to make an example of the young lady. We can't have the womenfolk come barging up here on a whim every time their feathers are up," Mr. Merriweather said.

The shame Kitty was going to feel when word got out that she'd crashed the Elks Club meeting was going to be something for the ages.

"Are you saying you want to press charges, Mer?" the officer asked.

"I am indeed," Mr. Merriweather said.

Becky felt a wave of distress pass over her, but then she thought of all the things they'd been saying about Judge.

"I'm ready, officer," Becky replied. "I'm not afraid to be judged for standing up for my father's honor when the men who call him their friend won't."

"All right. That's enough out of you. You're in enough trouble as it is."

The policeman pulled Becky out of the building. Every set of eyes was on her. She was terribly embarrassed and wondered if she shouldn't call Madame Cecelia to come to bail her out of the can. Maybe Nat would be willing to help.

"It isn't right what they were saying," she muttered as she looked around, hoping Teddy had seen her being loaded into the back of the police car. They hadn't slapped the cuffs on her, and she was grateful for that. But when the engine roared to life, the officer driving had no pity on her.

"What were you thinking, trying to muscle in on that group? It's just plain stupid if you ask me," he barked. "Now look at you. You're in a cop car, and I'm supposed to take you downtown to get your picture taken and your mitts blackened."

Becky had nothing to say. The copper wasn't in the mood to be sympathetic. And she was so angry at those men who called her father their friend that nothing ladylike was going to come out of her mouth.

"I'm trying to solve a murder," the police officer said. "One member of this community was snuffed out. He was fit for a Chicago overcoat under suspicious circumstances. He had a wife, even if she weren't faithful. Neither was he. It doesn't mean we ignore the facts, Miss. Not that a woman should even be bothering with such details. I find your snooping rather ghoulish to say the least."

Becky bounced along in the back seat, holding her tongue and trying to figure out what she was going to do once she was behind bars. Part of her wanted to cry and plead for the officer not to take her downtown. But another part of her was stubborn. Prideful. She had been standing up for her father. And what was Mr. Merriweather doing letting those men talk about Judge that way?

Just as she was steeling herself to face the judgmental eyes of the other officers, the car turned off the main route to downtown Savannah.

"I'll probably regret this, but I can't bring myself to deliver a young lady, no matter how ignorant she might be, to sit in a dirty cell with the regular riffraff," the officer said. "I have the feeling that your daddy, once I deliver you home, will have a just punishment to dole out."

"I think I'd rather go to the big house," Becky muttered.

"Don't be smart with me, young lady," the officer snapped.

"I'm sorry," Becky replied and gave a tired smile. "Thank you, Officer."

"Now, I want you to promise me I won't run into you trespassing, drinking at a speakeasy, or spitting on the sidewalk. Do you understand me?" he grumbled.

"Yes, sir," Becky answered as she looked at her family's house at the end of the long rows of tobacco plants.

There was no chance this copper would drop her off at the Old Brick Cemetery. Nor would he let her scale the trellis to sneak in. But if she did that, she'd be going back on her own promise to herself. She wasn't a kid anymore. Oh boy. If being brought home with a police escort didn't scream bad adult behavior, nothing did.

Just as the car came to a stop in front of the house, Kitty appeared. The look of worry on her face made Becky feel the air had been knocked out of her. She waited as the officer greeted Kitty with a firm "good evening."

"I believe this young lady belongs to you," the officer said as he opened the back door for Becky to step out.

"Rebecca! What in the world have you been up to?" Kitty demanded.

That brought Fanny outside. She gasped, her hand instantly to her mouth, but it was impossible for Becky to tell if Fanny was concerned or laughing at her.

"I was…"

"She was trespassing on private property, ma'am. The young people these days look for trouble." The officer sniffed and tugged the bottom of his coat, making the buttons glisten and erasing the wrinkles.

"Becky, where were you?"

"The Elks Club," Becky said. "I didn't know anyone was supposed to be there. Teddy had said his father was home tonight, and you know Mr. Rockdale never misses a meeting. Like Daddy never misses, and he wasn't…"

"Get inside this house right now. I've never been so embarrassed." Kitty snapped her fingers and pointed to the door.

Becky said nothing. She dropped her head and walked into the house. Why was everything backfiring against her? Nothing she could do was right or even worked out. What had she done that was so horrible that suddenly nothing was going her way?

"Officer, I do hope that this can end right here. I'll have a talk with my daughter, and you can bet that when her father comes home, there will be some changes around the house," Kitty said as she took a step closer to the edge of the porch.

"The head of the Elks, Mr. Merriweather, was very upset and talked of pressing charges," the officer said, making Becky wince as she heard the words.

"You've really done it now," Fanny whispered.

"Pipe down," Becky whispered back, making Fanny gasp.

"I think we can let this go *this time*. Your daughter and I already had a discussion on the way here. I don't think you'll be having any more problems. She knows what will happen if we cross paths again." The copper tipped his hat to Kitty.

"Oh, officer, thank you so much," Kitty replied. She waited until the policeman had turned his car around and was nothing more than a fading light in the distance.

When she walked into the house, Kitty found Becky sitting in the parlor on the edge of the bright-red velvet chair that was Becky's favorite.

"I don't know what to say," Kitty said.

"Mama, I went there for a reason. I heard those men who claim to be friends say…"

"I don't care, Becky. Please go to your room. I'll have to talk to your father about this when he gets home," Kitty replied.

"Where is he?" Becky never thought she'd ask

this, but even in the deep trouble she was in, all she wanted was to see her father. She'd explain everything, and he'd listen.

"Mr. Merriweather was there? He's going to tell Mrs. Merriweather that my daughter was scooped up by the authorities for trespassing. I won't be able to show my face in town for weeks." Kitty patted her hair nervously.

"Mama, if you'd just let me explain. Teddy and I…"

"Dear Lord, you brought Teddy into this too? Child, are you determined to ruin our good family name?" Kitty huffed. "The Rockdales don't need you contributing to the delinquency of their son."

"Where is Daddy? I'll talk to him. He'll listen!" Becky shouted.

Kitty kneaded her hands in front of her then slowly walked to her favorite chair, where a book sat on the table beneath a small Tiffany lamp.

"I don't know where your father is." Kitty looked as if the words were as sharp as glass and cut her mouth as she reluctantly spoke them.

"What do you mean you don't know where he is?" Becky asked, her worst fear forming into reality right in front of her.

Kitty looked at Becky then at the ground as if she were embarrassed. Humiliated was more like it.

"I don't know where he is. He doesn't tell me anymore."

Becky didn't move. It was as if a swarm of bees had just descended, and any sudden movement might result in her being stung to death. Even if she could move, what would she do? Where would she go? This wasn't anything Becky was prepared for. No matter what she was thinking or how much she had speculated that she might hear this horrible news, it still felt as if someone had picked her up and was dangling her over a big, empty black hole.

The house suddenly looked different, felt different. As if there was an invisible intruder inside. Becky did the only thing she could. She got up from her seat, went to her mother, and, for the first time in her whole life, offered *her* shoulder for Kitty to cry on. And Kitty did.

Becky held her mother and forced herself not to shed a single tear. Kitty needed her to be strong right now. This was no time to ask questions, to make assumptions, or to speculate about what was really going on. They would all know eventually. The truth had a way of charging into the middle of everything whether anyone wanted it to or not.

"Oh, dear. I've gone and ruined my face powder," Kitty remarked as she leaned back and wiped her tears. When she looked at Becky, Becky forced a little smile.

"You still look real pretty, Mama," she replied.

Kitty kissed her on the cheek and patted her bright-red hair. "You go on to bed. Let's not talk about tonight until after we've had a good night's sleep," Kitty said.

Becky nodded, gave her mother one more squeeze, then went up the stairs to her bedroom.

Fanny was waiting at the top of the staircase. "Brought home by the police? Cousin Rebecca, I sometimes wonder how we can be related," Fanny said just barely over a whisper.

"I ask myself that all the time," Becky snapped back.

"And I don't know what you and Aunt Kitty are making such a fuss about. I told you that when I was in Paris, I discovered that almost every man had a mistress. You were considered a flat tire if you didn't have one." Fanny shrugged as she walked down the hallway with Becky.

"Have you said any of that nonsense to Mama?" Becky hissed.

"Not yet. But I was thinking of broaching the

topic with her soon. Just to put her mind at ease. In fact, women in Paris also often take lovers too…"

"Don't you dare talk to her about anything you learned in Paris, you got that? Or I'll make sure you fade, and fast," Becky said as she cornered Fanny against the wall.

"You really are very unladylike." Fanny huffed before she went to her room and shut the door firmly.

That blond bombshell had no idea how close she'd come to having those pretty blue eyes replaced with googs. A couple of shiners might be just what she needed, Becky thought.

Becky stood in the hallway for a few seconds as her legs trembled and her heart raced. She went to her room and quietly closed the door tight. Once she was alone, she started to cry. She wept quietly for just a few minutes. Then she stopped and thought about what it was she was going to do about this situation.

Just because those men at the Elks had nasty things to say about Judge Mackenzie didn't meant they were at all true. And there was one woman in town who had the skinny on just about everyone: Elizabeth Gilmore.

CHAPTER FIFTEEN

The next day, Becky ran next door to the Rockdales' house to find Teddy reading a book on his front porch with a mint julep in his hand. When he saw Becky approaching, he smiled but shook his head.

"I saw you loaded into that paddy wagon and was sure I was going to have to fork over a mint to get you out of the cooler," he said before looking over his shoulder at the house to make sure no one was listening. "How much trouble are you in?"

"I'm not sure," Becky replied, which was the truth.

"I followed you, but when I saw that the copper was bringing you home, I figured you'd be all right.

You don't look like you are any worse for wear." Teddy gave her a gentle tap on the chin. "Trouble's been on your heels lately."

"I know," Becky said sadly.

Everyone in her house knew something wasn't right. The air inside was filled with tension, and it seemed to keep getting thicker with every passing day. Judge had come home late last night and had spoken to no one. Kitty had gotten up early, but she spoke to no one. Fanny spoke to anyone who would listen about her desperate need for a new dress and how she'd been thinking that it might be time for Aunt Kitty and Uncle Judge to throw another party.

"The weather is deliciously cool," Fanny said. "I think after the luncheon excitement, it might be a nice way to show our appreciation to our friends and neighbors."

Kitty nodded and said she'd think about it. Becky felt awful for her mother. But still, she wasn't going to put her emotions on display as she had in the past. Even if she was spitting mad, she was going to hold her head high.

"Whose friends and neighbors?" Becky asked.

"Why, *our* friends and neighbors." Fanny glared at Becky, who took a long sip of coffee.

Now at Teddy's she asked him for help. She should have known he'd be a little hesitant. How many times had she dragged him on a wild goose chase in which he'd gotten into a pinch? Too many times.

"Forget it. I'll ask Moxley. I'm sure he needs something in town," Becky said. "You know I adore you, Teddy. And I'm sorry for all the hoopla."

"Oh, you know that I can't say no to you. Let me get my hat," Teddy said, making Becky feel relieved.

"I mean it," she said as they drove. "You are the cat's pajamas. And you can just drop me off at the bank. I'll walk from there."

"Where are you headed?" Teddy asked. "Because I don't think Adam is able to leave work today. I wouldn't even try to hunt him down."

Becky was surprised when she looked at Teddy. "What? I wasn't going to look for Adam, but why would you say that?"

"I just didn't want you wearing your dogs out if he wasn't around," Teddy said, but Becky didn't need a death row confession to know he was not telling her the whole story.

"Teddy, is there something you're not telling me?" Becky asked.

"Of course not, doll. You said drop you at the bank? I can do that." He hit the gas, and the car swerved and jostled them both as he handled the corners and zipped around the slower jalopies.

Becky didn't say anything more until he pulled the car to a stop in front of the bank.

"Be honest. Do you need me to come and pick you up?" Teddy asked with his straw hat cocked to the side.

"No. I brought cab fare home," Becky said, giving him a peck on the cheek. "And don't think I won't find out what you're hiding. Martha is my best friend. And I know what she's like after a couple of champagne cocktails."

Teddy didn't reply as he watched her climb out of the car, but Becky was sure he looked concerned. But she had other things to worry about. Dropping in on Mrs. Gilmore unannounced was not only unladylike but against all forms of Southern etiquette. If she'd been kin, it would have been okay. But they were barely acquaintances, and for all Becky knew, the old woman might just slam the door in her face. Still, Becky had to try. Sitting around and waiting for things to unfold was not what Becky wanted to do.

From the bank, if she walked two blocks up and seven blocks over, she'd be in a quaint little area in which some of Savannah's older homes were located. Mrs. Gilmore lived in a rather large house, where she rented out the rooms to gentlemen and the occasional lady passing through town. With a three-dollar deposit up front, she was able to give herself a comfortable life. She'd never be wealthy like the Merriweathers or the Mackenzies for that matter. But everyone knew if they needed a room, a good meal, and a clean place to stay, Mrs. Gilmore's was the place to go.

Of course, there were some people who didn't care for her operation. They thought she wasn't discriminating enough with her tenants. But Becky wondered who else would tend to these people and help them get a leg up if not Mrs. Gilmore. One didn't see Mrs. Merriweather out there bringing blankets and dinner to those in the bread line.

the house was on the corner. A weather-worn sign off the sidewalk read Gilmore—Rooms for Rent. The white-and-blue paint that framed the shutters was chipped and faded. But the flowers growing around her home were beautiful tiger lilies, and several rosebushes heavy with blooms clung protectively to the house. It looked like a happy place, and suddenly Becky didn't feel so concerned about whether she was being ladylike or proper.

She walked up the sidewalk and pressed the buzzer. She could hear the gritty chirp inside, and within seconds, footsteps on a hardwood floor came to the door. The Irish lace that hung over an oval window was pulled aside, and Mrs. Gilmore peeked out. She smiled immediately. With a strong yank and a creak of the hinges, the door opened wide.

"Why, Rebecca Mackenzie. This is a surprise," Mrs. Gilmore said happily.

She had a dingy white towel over her shoulder on which she wiped her hands. Becky had only seen her on a few occasions around the other old hens, and the woman never smiled. In fact, she played rather daft in a simple house dress like the one she was wearing now and with her hair a little out of place like it was now. She ran what the other women called a flophouse. Really, from what Becky could see, it was much nicer than that and rather cozy.

"Hi, Mrs. Gilmore."

"What are you doing all the way over here? This is an old part of town. A pretty girl your age should be in the thick of it down at the department store or the beauty shop." Mrs. Gilmore giggled.

"Mrs. Gilmore, I'm really sorry to bother you."

"No bother. I love visitors. Come on in. I just put on a pot of coffee for Mr. Talbot. Would you like a cup?"

"That would be lovely. Yes, thank you," Becky said as she followed the woman down a long hallway into her kitchen.

It was nothing like her home's grand kitchen with Lucretia bustling about from one side to the other, darting in and out of a pantry that was as big as this room. But it had a wonderfully warm feel to it. The table in the middle was clean and had a porcelain salt and pepper set in the middle. None of the chairs matched. The tablecloth had huge orange and yellow peaches and bright-red cherries on it. There was more Irish lace hanging from the kitchen window that let in just enough light and fresh air to keep it as cool as a Southern kitchen could be.

"Mr. Talbot has been with me for years. A very loyal friend he's become. Every day, he likes one last cup of coffee around ten o'clock. So don't mind him when he comes shuffling through," Mrs. Gilmore said with a smile.

She put a steaming cup of joe in front of Becky and one for herself after she set one cup on the counter and left it there. Obviously, it was for Mr. Talbot.

"Mrs. Gilmore, I have to ask you a question. And I do hope you don't find me out of sorts. But it has to do with the pie contest," Becky said. She watched Mrs. Gilmore's eyes take on a sad shadow.

"That was a tragedy. And I know it isn't very Christian of me, but I had perfected my recipe. I was going to shock everyone. Especially those two biddies who act like they've been commissioned by the pope in Rome to win every year," Mrs. Gilmore said.

"You must be talking about Mrs. Hindergast and Mrs. Brower." Becky smirked.

"That's them," Mrs. Gilmore replied, shaking her head. "I never said I was the world's greatest baker. But I overheard them two years ago at the competition saying that they'd rather eat dirt than have to taste my pie. Eat dirt, they said. And then they laughed."

"Oh, Mrs. Gilmore, I'm so sorry." Becky saw the old woman's eyes glisten as the pain of those comments still stung.

"Ain't your fault, honey." Mrs. Gilmore blinked and smiled. "But I did hear that they were beside themselves when the pies were all ruined by Mr. Foxworthy's untimely accident. I'm not sure what I would have liked better, getting the blue ribbon or watching their game of high hat getting cut short."

Becky chuckled. But when she took a sip of her coffee, she almost began to cough. It was the worst coffee she'd ever tasted—bitter and thick with bits of grounds still floating around.

"Mrs. Gilmore, who do you think put the poison in their pie? I don't believe it was Natalie Phine, the new lady from town," Becky said.

"Oh, she is a peach, isn't she?" Mrs. Gilmore said.

"You've met her?" Becky replied. "I don't think the stories about her are true, either. It's hard to know."

"She is quite a character. No, I don't believe she had anything to do with it. But to be honest with you, I'm not sure Mr. Foxworthy didn't do it to himself. He had a bad ticker. He also was suffering from a rather bad case of...one of those nasty diseases," Mrs. Gilmore whispered.

"Oh my!" Becky gasped. "How do you know this?"

"You'd be surprised at what people will talk about when they think you are so old your hearing is going. I know a lot more than they'll ever know." She winked and made Becky smile.

She suddenly caught a strong smell of Aqua Velva

with an undertone of body odor that struck her for a moment, causing her to reach for the cup of bad coffee and choke down another gulp in order to be polite. When she then looked at the counter, Becky realized the cup Mrs. Gilmore had put there was gone.

"Mr. Talbot came for his coffee," Mrs. Gilmore said quietly.

"Well, he is light on his loafers. I didn't hear so much as a floorboard squeak. But then again, I guess that's the kind of tenant you want. A quiet one," Becky joked.

"That's the problem with people today. They talk-talk-talk. Sometimes it's nice to keep a little mystery to yourself. People don't need to know where your family comes from or what you do for a living. They should be more concerned with how you act, don't you think?" Mrs. Gilmore asked Becky.

"Yes, well, I'm afraid I don't speak or act all that well, according to some of the people in this town," Becky replied. "My father hasn't been speaking to me very much, and he and I were thick as thieves my whole life."

"Judge Mackenzie," Mrs. Gilmore said softly.

"Yes, ma'am."

"He's a fine man. An honorable man. I wouldn't believe anything unfavorable anyone said about him. I've run into Judge on more than one occasion. A gentleman through and through," Mrs. Gilmore said with her chin raised.

"So you haven't heard any rumors about him and anyone stepping out?" Becky felt a lump in her throat but choked it back.

"I have not," she said sadly, shaking her head.

"Okay. Well, I do appreciate your time, Mrs. Gilmore." Becky took her last gulp of coffee and swallowed it quickly so as not to let the burned taste and tiny substances have time to linger in her mouth.

"I enjoyed the visit, young lady. I think what we ought to do is get Mrs. Natalie Phine and yourself together to have a good old-fashioned sewing bee. Minus the sewing," Mrs. Gilmore said and then giggled cheerfully.

"I think that sounds wonderful," Becky replied.

Already, Becky was making a plan in her head of when to bring Nat and Martha to Mrs. Gilmore's boarding house. It would be great fun, and maybe, just maybe, Kitty would like to join them. Becky thought her mother would do well to meet Nat. And as far as Becky knew, she had never spent any time getting to know Mrs. Gilmore. All Kitty knew about her was what she'd heard, and that was that she ran a boarding house and was rather lax about who lived beneath her roof.

"And I'm going to make another pie with the recipe I perfected. Then you can have a taste and tell those old biddies that my pie was tastier, and that they wouldn't have won the contest," Mrs. Gilmore said. "That would knock their noses out of joint, don't you think?"

"Yes. I'll make sure you are with me when I say it," Becky said. Again, she shook Mrs. Gilmore's hand and thanked her for her hospitality. On her way out, she heard the squeaking of boards coming from upstairs. Of course she did. There were people up there. Not everyone worked in a tobacco field from sunup to sunset.

Becky left Mrs. Gilmore's house feeling better. Still, her father was acting strangely, and she was determined to get to the bottom of it first. Mrs. Merriweather had probably left skid marks on the sidewalk when she tore out of her home that morning to tell the other ladies that Kitty Mackenzie's daughter had been picked up by the police the previous evening.

At least she knew that not everyone was under

the spell of the Merriweathers of the world. Neither Mrs. Gilmore nor Nat had anything to do with them. Even Cecelia kept them at arm's length. And with the mere thought of her friend, Becky swallowed her pride and headed off to 784½ Bryn Mawr.

CHAPTER SIXTEEN

*A*s soon as Becky pushed open the door to the apothecary, the sweet tinkling of bells sounded. Becky didn't know why, but she felt her heart in her throat. She'd gotten mad at Cecelia for not telling her what her tarot reading meant, and as she stepped across the threshold, it suddenly seemed like a childish and horrible way to treat her friend.

Ophelia, Cecelia's mother, looked up from her perch on a chair, where she was reading, her one white eye looking judgmentally at the visitor. But as quick as a flash, she jumped off the stool and raced around the counter. Her white hair was in a bun, but thin wisps had fallen around her face, and for a brief second, as the shadow of a tall display covered her

185

slightly, Becky thought she looked like an angel. But she didn't know why Ophelia was racing toward her and put up her hands defensively.

"What? What is it?" Becky exclaimed, rousing the attention of the two patrons who were perusing Ophelia's exotic herbs and trinkets.

It was amazing that no matter what time of day or night, Becky always spotted customers in the store. They'd slink in, barely speak, look for their love potions or charms to ward off the evil eye or special candles that would bring financial success, cure a case of rickets, or chase away termites, and pay handsomely for it all. Then they'd leave.

"Rebecca! Where have you been?" Ophelia wrapped her skinny arms around Becky and squeezed her so tightly that Becky was sure there would be bruises on her skin tomorrow.

"Around?" Becky replied.

"Go upstairs now. Cecelia has been waiting for you. She misses you. It makes her crabby and terrible to be around. Only room for one crabby lady in this place," she said as she jerked her thumb at her own chest. "Go now." With a gentle shove, Ophelia directed Becky to the stairs behind the counter that led to their apartment above the store.

As soon as Becky started to ascend the familiar set of stairs, she felt the presence of so many of Cecelia's relatives that it was as if a warm, invisible blanket had wrapped around her. Even Cousin Mimi, a devious spirit who, according to her kin, had been miserable in life and continued to be in the afterlife, didn't trip up Becky's steps or give her a shove from behind. Once at the top of the landing, Becky gently knocked on the door.

"Come in, Becky," Cecelia softly said.

"Tell her!" Ophelia shouted from downstairs, her shrill voice making Becky jump.

"Mother!"

"If you don't tell her, you'll be plagued by ants!" Ophelia continued.

"She's been telling me I'll be plagued by ants since I was ten years old," Cecelia said from the stove, where she was lifting a steaming kettle off the burner.

"Yikes." Becky shuddered. "And I thought being told I'd never get invited to any of the good parties was a threat."

Cecelia chuckled as she motioned for Becky to take a seat at the little table by the window and the garden growing on the fire escape. The fresh air blew in, cool and soft. Becky took her seat and immediately noticed the deck of tarot cards.

"Becky, I owe you an apology," Cecelia started.

"No. I owe you an apology. I acted like a spoiled brat who didn't get her way. That's just plain rude, and as my mother would say, I was raised better than that." Becky rolled her eyes before she sat down.

Cecelia poured their tea, put the kettle back on the stove, and then took her seat. Becky reached across the table and took Cecelia's hand.

"We are not like everyone else. That can be a blessing and a curse. I thought that if I didn't tell you your future, I'd be protecting you. I even said that I learned the hard way that trying to hide what the cards say only brings more trouble. You've been having trouble, haven't you?" Cecelia squeezed Becky's hand.

In that instant, Becky began to cry. "I don't even know where to start."

"Oh, I feel like this is my fault. I should have told you everything. Tell me, what's the skinny been at your house?" Cecelia asked.

Becky took a deep breath and rattled off all the stress that had been piling on over the past few days.

"Ever since the fair, Cecelia. I missed my father's performance with the Elks' Jolly Corks, and my mother was beside herself. Then there was the death, and I was sure I spotted the culprit. But my father has ties to him. And he and my mother aren't talking like they usually do. And with this murder hanging out there, all signs are pointing to my old man. And then there was the issue at the Elks Club, and word will undoubtedly get back to Mrs. Merriweather, who has never had a kind word to say about me. Then Fanny said affairs are normal and…"

"You poor dear. Okay, let's face the music." Cecelia shuffled the cards and laid them out across the table. There were many familiar designs facing Becky. They were almost the same as she had seen that day at the fair.

"Is it all the same as before? It's all the same as before, isn't it? Am I doomed? I'm doomed, aren't I?" Becky asked nervously, sniffing back tears.

"All right, let's get out from behind the eight ball," Cecelia said. She took a deep breath and looked at Becky. "I see someone leaving. It is a man."

"It's my father, isn't it? He's been acting strange. He's been out of the house and not coming home for hours at a time. My mama says he isn't talking to her, and he certainly isn't speaking to me. Oh, and there are people talking around town who say that he's been stepping out and…"

"It's Adam," Cecelia said.

"What?"

"The man who is leaving you is Adam," Cecelia said apologetically.

"That can't be right." Becky's eyes dried up, and she was more angry than sad. "I don't understand. I haven't seen him in a couple days, but the last time I saw him, things were ducky."

"I see the influence of another woman. He doesn't love her. But, honey, he doesn't love you either, or he wouldn't have stepped out on you," Cecelia said. "But that isn't all I see. There is a lot more. Now let's look at…"

"I don't believe this. I wonder if that's what set Teddy off the other night. He's gone sour on Adam, but no one would tell me why. I'm not a child, Cecelia." Becky looked up at her friend. "I can handle bad news. What did everyone think I was going to do? Tie a rock around my neck and throw myself off a bridge?"

"You are loved by so many people, Becky. You have no idea. That's half of what I see in these cards. It isn't all bad news here. In fact, I see…"

"Who does he think he is? I mean, he's a Yankee after all." Becky couldn't believe what she was saying. She sounded just like her mother. "After all the trouble I went through to get my parents to accept him. And they did. Mostly. Kitty was still a little hesitant, but she let him in the house. She didn't point a mohaska at him, I'll tell you that much. And what in the world did he do to Teddy to get him to react the way he did?"

"I don't know." Cecelia took a sip of her own cup of tea. Before she could continue her reading, Becky gasped, her eyes bulged, and she put her hand up to her face.

"That had to be what put a bee in Teddy's bonnet. He knew. And if he knew, Martha knew. They didn't say anything to me. Why wouldn't they tell me, Cecelia?" Becky shook her head.

"The same reason I didn't. I'd hoped you'd discover it on your own. But when I shuffle the cards for a person and then try and manipulate them or conceal what the universe is unfolding, it causes more harm than good. The universe will push the horrible truth in your face like a pie," Cecelia said.

"I feel like my parents have been the main thing to focus on." Becky huffed. Suddenly she stopped speaking and looked down at her lap. She hadn't seen Adam in a couple of days. She'd been so concerned about her parents that there hadn't been room for anything else.

"Take a sip of tea and relax. Let me see what else I can see," Cecelia soothed.

Becky did as she was told and took a deep breath. She was angry, but the tea was a magical elixir that instantly calmed her nerves. Whether or not it was a special potion, Becky didn't know, but she quickly took another sip.

"Now, I also see a big change coming your way. I see a lot more room. Something big will be changing the way you live," Cecelia said.

"Oh my gosh, is Fanny leaving? Please tell me Fanny is leaving. She's found a richer, more desperate relative who wants the company. Oh, that would make all of this worth it." Becky clapped and wiped the last of her tears from her eyes.

"I don't know if that's it. All I see is a lot of space. And it is a good thing," Cecelia said.

"Now what about my parents? Can you tell me if they will work things out? My mama won't be a fire alarm, will she? Divorced?" Becky wrung her hands.

"I'm sorry, Becky. I can't see their future. I don't know how things are going to pan out for them. But if you can bring them here, I'll be glad to do a reading for them." Cecelia smiled. "But, Becky, one more thing that I see for you. This card with the owl and shield." She tapped the picture with her smooth red nail.

"Is it bad?" Becky asked.

"No. Don't look for the negative all the time, Becky, because it will find you. It will find you and dig in deep," Cecelia said. "This symbolizes the wealth of wise and wonderful people who are around you, not only looking to come to your rescue but waiting for you to come to theirs too. You might be the bull in the China shop, but those who know you are grateful for that. They wouldn't want you any other way."

Becky smiled.

"Now, you have many challenges facing you, and they aren't going to get wrapped up in a neat little bow. And I shouldn't have to remind you that some of your friends are in a position to help in a more spectral capacity. They need to earn their right to pass over. That is their ticket. Punch it for them." Cecelia smiled. "Oh, and I also see someone who has a very angelic face, but be careful. I don't know if it's a man or a woman. But they are just out for themselves, and you might be in the way."

Becky thanked Cecelia. Once the cards had been scooped up into a neat stack and slipped back into the purple velvet sack with a drawstring tie at the top, Becky and Cecelia had another cup of tea and chatted pleasantly.

"So, tell me why you had to be brought home in a paddy wagon." Cecelia smirked as she pulled a cold bottle of suds from her fridge and handed it to Becky.

"How do you know about that?" Becky squinted at Cecelia suspiciously.

"It was in the cards." Cecelia chuckled.

"At least you didn't hear it from Mrs. Merri-weather. You better grab yourself a bottle if you want to hear this story." Becky laughed too.

"It's my mother's beer," Cecelia said.

"Are you sure I should be drinking it?" Becky asked before taking her first gulp.

"Sure, what's the worst that could happen?"

"I'll be plagued by ants," Becky replied.

She spent the afternoon chatting with Cecelia and sipping drinks. Even though she'd gotten news that was bad, or mysterious to say the least, she felt lighter than she had in days. Finally, it felt as if the world had righted itself. Things might not be the same; they might even be heartbreaking if what Cecelia had said was true. But as Becky left the apartment and waved good-bye to Ophelia, who was haggling with a man over a jingling necklace, she felt her feet firmly on the ground. Things were going to be different. She could tell.

Within minutes, she was in a cab on her way home. When she got there, Fanny was pacing on the porch. Becky was ready.

CHAPTER SEVENTEEN

*T*he cab dropped Becky off at the end of the long dirt road that was her driveway. As much as she wanted not to believe what Cecelia had said about Adam, she knew that it had to be true. Cecelia would have no reason to make up some kind of story just to cause trouble between them. As she walked, she kicked the dirt, and the red dust puffed up around her ankles, coating her Mary Janes. She had to ask Adam if it was true. It was as simple as that. Sure, she could go running to Teddy, who would probably confirm the whole thing, and Martha as well. But she had to hear Adam say it. That was what a real lady would do.

As she approached the porch, Fanny was sitting

on the front swing with her shoes off and a tall lemonade on the side table.

"It's about time you got home. Your daddy was looking for you. You were supposed to join him out in the tobacco field today but were nowhere to be found," Fanny said with a simp of satisfaction on her face. She had a fashion magazine in her lap and lazily licked her finger to turn a page.

"Don't you have something else to do?" Becky snapped as she started to go up the porch steps.

"You might want to cheese it and shimmy up the trellis like you usually do." Fanny rolled her eyes. "Once Aunt Kitty gets a hold of you, I don't think you'll be joining Martha and Teddy tonight at the fair."

"How do you know they are going to the fair?" Becky asked as she climbed the stairs, ready to enter her home through the front door.

"Teddy stopped by here. He said he drove you to town and had thought you'd be home by now. He asked me to give you a message that they were going to Willie's tonight, and we are both invited. He is just the sweetest thing. There weren't many men in Paris like him. Don't get me wrong; the gentlemen were more than plentiful. Well, for a woman of fine taste. But he really is one of a kind," Fanny purred.

It drove Becky crazy to hear her talk like that about Teddy. He was like a brother, and if Fanny thought she was going to sink her claws into him and make him more miserable than a mattress full of bedbugs, she had another thing coming.

But then Becky thought about Adam. Teddy knew what he'd done. Becky had no idea how he knew, but he did. He had been willing to take on that big palooka because he thought of Becky as his sister.

"You're right, Fanny. He really is one of a kind," Becky replied and went inside the house to face whatever trouble she was in.

"Becky, is that you?" Kitty shouted from upstairs.

"Yes, Mama," Becky called up the stairs. She took off her shoes to hide them behind her back, but it was no use. The dust had left a perfect imprint on her feet. It looked as if she was still wearing shoes except they were skin colored. Becky wanted to talk to her mother and see how things were going. But as soon as she stepped into her mother's room, her heart stopped.

"Mama, what are you doing?"

"Your Aunt Verona sent word that her mother-in-law was suffering terrible from a bout of ague. Although no one has taken her temperature to know for sure," Kitty said as she packed a few things into a suitcase.

"When will you be back?"

"Just a few days, dear. Please, do me a favor. Tend to your father. Do as he asks, and don't cause him any unnecessary problems. You were supposed to join him in the field today. I told him you had an engagement that you couldn't get out of." Kitty cleared her throat as she packed a few more things.

"Thanks. Would you like me to come with you?" Becky took a step closer. As soon as she did, Kitty saw her feet and started to chuckle.

"No. I know you don't care for Aunt Verona. Truthfully, neither do I. But when family needs you..." Kitty shrugged and closed the suitcase and snapped it shut.

"Is Moxley driving you to the train station? I'll go with you," Becky offered, but her mother shook her head.

"No. Martha's mama will be here any minute. She's driving me, since it's not far past Poole County. I do believe she'll be dropping Martha off. Something about all of you going out again tonight." Kitty looked in the mirror and patted her finger curls nervously like she always did.

"Yeah, that's what Fanny said." Becky cleared her throat. "When will Daddy be home?"

"Later this evening, I suppose. He's got a lot on his mind." Kitty smiled weakly.

"I suppose he does." Becky squared her shoulders and held back tears for her mother's sake.

After looking around the room, she saw that many of her mother's most beloved things were still there. A favorite picture of Becky when she was a baby, her statue of Mother Mary, and a photo of her and Judge on their wedding day were all still in their proper places. And after a quick glance, Becky saw that Kitty's beautiful wedding band still sparkled on her ring finger.

Before Becky could say another word, the sound of a car pulling up the drive distracted her. She walked up and took the suitcase from her mother and offered to carry it downstairs.

Just as she reached the bottom of the steps, Martha came inside with Fanny right behind her. "I don't know if Becky will be permitted to go. She's been on an awful tangent, causing all sorts of…"

"Martha, dear!" Becky cried.

"Miss Rebecca!" Martha replied in kind. "So good of you to invite me to your humble dwelling. Where's the hooch?"

"Shh. In the parlor. Give me a couple minutes." Becky winked as she put on her best performance of hiding her real feelings. She slipped out the front door, paying no attention to Fanny, and gently placed her mother's suitcase in the back seat of the Bourdeauxes' Studebaker. It was their second automobile.

"Becky, darling. You are looking wonderful. Oh, I especially love your new stockings. Is that the rage these days?" Mrs. Bourdeaux teased as she waited behind the wheel for Kitty.

Becky smiled and shook her head before giving Mrs. Bourdeaux a kiss on the cheek. "That's what I get for kicking up dust." Becky shrugged innocently.

"Don't you worry about your mama, now. We'll be back in a couple days. I hear you all are going to the fair. The big fireworks are tomorrow night. That was always my favorite part. Will you and Adam be attending together?" Mrs. Bourdeaux asked.

"I'm sure something will be arranged," Becky replied.

Thankfully, her mother appeared and quickly hurried down the porch steps. Becky ran to her side of the car and kissed her mother on the cheek. Before she could climb in, Becky hugged Kitty tightly and told her she loved her more than anything.

"Why, Becky. You're acting like I'm joining the French Foreign Legion. I'll only be gone a few days." Kitty smiled and kissed her daughter on the cheek.

Within just a few minutes, Becky was walking up the porch steps. Martha greeted her with a gin fizzy.

"Here you are, darling. Bottoms up." They clinked their glasses and took a sip. Fanny had put on a record before they all gathered in the parlor.

"So, I hear the fair is on the list of things to do," Becky said, enjoying her drink and looking forward to the next one.

"Oh yes. And I've already made plans with Teddy that we will all be going to Racy Jack's Club 360." Martha batted her lashes.

"Oh no. Not that clip joint." Becky put her hand to her cheek. "The music is awful, and the drinks are watered down. Why anyone would willingly go to that place I'm sure I don't know."

"I've got us an in. The woman who does my nails is a canary there. She's already set us up at a table. Since when do you and I worry about watered-down drinks? We'll get one glass to share, and the refills will be provided by the Flask Sisters." Martha winked, making Becky chuckle.

"What's wrong with Racy Jack's?" Fanny called out over the music.

"Oh, you'll fit right in. There are lots of butter-and-egg men there. Do you have a nice dress to wear?" Becky replied.

"Do I? Of course I do." Fanny rolled her eyes as if a sillier question couldn't have been asked. It made Becky and Martha chuckle.

The ladies spent a pleasant afternoon talking about anything and everything, but it was impossible for the conversation not to turn to the murder of Clem Foxworthy.

"Have the police said anything more?" Becky asked. She'd told Martha about her visit to Mrs. Gilmore and how that old biddy had been as pleasant as punch on a hot summer day. "Now I know why Hindergast and Brower don't like her. She's gone the opposite way of Nat Phine. Instead of having the strong bucks beating a path to her door, she's got the old timers down on their luck. Both of those ladies are a heck of a lot more interesting than the rest of the hens in town."

"That will be us someday, Rebecca. You'll be fighting off the brunos, and I'll be tending the winos." Martha giggled before taking another sip of her drink.

"I don't know why you'd want to associate with either one of them," Fanny griped as she emerged from her bedroom, where she'd been changing for the evening's events. She was wearing a pink number with a headband. There was no way she could be missed. Becky thought she looked like a flamingo.

"You'd be surprised, Fanny," Martha replied. "Some of those old ladies are the best bootleggers in town. Why, I would be surprised if Mrs. Gilmore didn't have five bathtubs in her basement filled with gin."

"That's why she's got a stable of regular tenants." Becky laughed.

She'd had a couple glasses of giggle juice, and although she wasn't hung, she was feeling good. When Teddy showed up, Becky said goodbye to Lucretia without inquiring about her father. She was having real fun. It felt like it had been one hundred years since she had. She didn't want to ruin it. And as an extra bonus, pulling up behind Teddy was Stephen Penbroke.

"Well, I'll be a monkey's uncle," Becky gasped.

Her smile was genuine, as she was fond of Stephen. He had some designs on her that he'd made rather apparent, but Becky just couldn't bring herself to feel that way toward him. Of course, he was a handsome hombre and had a heavy wallet, but there was just that certain something missing. The thing she felt for Adam just wasn't there. And now that she was going out, wearing her best duds and surrounded by her good friends and Fanny, Becky felt a pang in her heart. Quickly, she shoved it aside.

"Why, Stephen Penbroke, you devil!" Fanny nearly broke her ankles running in her heels to get to the man before Becky could. She wrapped him in a big hug before she linked her arm through his. "Where in the world have you been hiding yourself?"

"Hello, Fanny. I've been spreading it around." He let out a whistle. "My goodness, Rebecca. You do look pretty tonight. Adam will have to fight them off with a whip and a chair."

Becky looked at Stephen suspiciously before she turned to Teddy, who cleared his throat and hopped out of his flivver to get the door for Martha.

"We outta breeze before they run out of ice," Teddy said. "Uh, Fanny. Come on and join Martha and me. Stephen, old chap, you wouldn't mind giving a lift to a dame like Becky, would you?"

"It would be my pleasure," Stephen replied as he walked Fanny to Teddy's car before he opened the door of his car for Becky. It was like musical chairs.

She flopped down in the front seat, smirked, and folded her arms.

"We'll see you at Racy Jacks!" Martha shouted, waving a kerchief as they turned the car around and whizzed past.

"Why do I get the feeling this was arranged?" Becky asked as they sped along the street.

Stephen was an excellent driver, but still, he managed to hit every red light. It was more than obvious he was trying to spend as much time alone with Becky as possible.

"Don't think for one second I've given up on you, Rebecca Mackenzie. I just thought if I held back a little, you might get to missing me. So?"

"So what?" Becky played.

"So, did you miss me?" Stephen asked.

"I wouldn't say I missed you. But I noticed you weren't around. Sort of like the time I got poison ivy. One day, it just wasn't as annoying as it had been, and before I knew it, it was gone."

"Is that so?"

"Yes. I'm sure you heard about the murder in town." She quickly changed the subject.

"I was never a fan of blueberry pie. But you can bet I won't be eating any now. What do you know about the fella it happened to?" Stephen asked.

"Clem Foxworthy? Not much. He was a member of the Elks Club with my father. He had a reputation for being a man about town. I don't think his wife liked it very much, but she had her own reputation. It's all rather seedy, and I don't really want to talk about it," Becky said as they pulled up to a parking spot about two blocks from Racy Jack's. She recalled her father whispering to Bernice at the Mackenzie estate, and it made her stomach fold over on itself.

"You'd have to really hate someone to go through such an elaborate plan to kill them with poison. Especially in a public place," Stephen said as he helped Becky out of the car. They began to walk down the sidewalk toward Racy Jack's.

"Well, hell hath no fury. That's what they say," Becky replied.

"Look, I might be talking out of line, but I'd never do something like that. Not just to you," Stephen said as he offered her his arm. When she wrapped her hand around his elbow, Stephen placed his other hand over hers. "I don't have it in me. I'm not a two-timer."

"Yeah, tell it to your Aunt Tilly." Becky smirked.

"It's true. When I see something that I want, I get it. And I take care of it." He raised his chin proudly.

"I don't know. Some people might say a man who

brags about his faithfulness is trying to cover for his lack of faithfulness," Becky teased.

It was obvious that Teddy had told him about Adam. She couldn't say she wasn't enjoying the attention. The past couple of days had been about everyone else. Clem Foxworthy. Judge. Kitty. Madame Cecelia. The ladies who had entered their pies in the pie-baking contest. Fanny. Teddy. And finally Adam. Stephen was a breath of fresh air.

"You might just have to take a leap of faith. If you can set your selfish ways aside for just a minute," Stephen said. At least, Becky thought he said those cruel words. She stopped and looked at him. That was when she saw it: a strange blur over his face that made him look like a photo out of focus for just a second. Then it was gone.

"What did you say?" Becky huffed.

"I said you might just have to take a leap of faith. If you don't mind being the dish at my side at this gin joint," Stephen said with an adorable smile.

"Can I tell you something?" Becky asked. She expected Stephen to make some kind of silly comment, but he didn't. In fact, he didn't say anything but looked at her and nodded.

Becky took a deep breath and told him about the hallucinations she was having. That they'd started when she'd missed her father's show at the fair and hadn't stopped. Then she said what she thought she'd heard him say, and a look of concern spread across his face.

"First of all, Becky, I'd never say such a thing—not just because I'm not that kind of person but because you are one of the kindest people I know. I think you might be expecting people to judge you harshly because they always have. I know your mother wants you to settle down with a fine fellow and get married. I know the ladies in town see you as strange. So maybe after all this time of pretending it doesn't bother you, it's bubbling over that maybe it does a little," Stephen said as they continued their walk.

"You don't think I'm losing my marbles?" Becky asked.

"You might be. But right now, you look as sane as Father Gerard at the pulpit in St. Jerome's on Sunday," Stephen said.

"You do have a way of making me laugh." Becky smiled and felt better. "Maybe you are right. I'm not saying you are. But it's a thought. I'll chew on it for a while."

As they neared Racy Jack's, they could hear the sound of music from inside. The rest of the gang was waiting for them at the door.

"Hey, slowpokes. What took you so long? Come on. The ice is melting," Teddy said as he held the door open.

After she crossed the threshold, Becky felt the electricity of the place and couldn't wait to get out on the dance floor. True to her word, Martha's friend had reserved a table for them just steps from the stage. They piled in, and within seconds, everyone had a drink. The music was jumping. The girls were twirling around, their bobs flying up like the hems of their dresses. Becky was feeling great. As she sipped her watered-down gin and tonic, which Martha had already topped off with hooch from her flask, she saw a familiar face at the bar.

"Martha! Do you see who that is at the bar?" Becky shouted in her friend's ear.

Martha looked and finally saw exactly who Becky was talking about. "I don't believe it!"

There at the bar was Lucille Clementine.

CHAPTER EIGHTEEN

*T*he bar in Racy Jack's was packed three people deep. It was almost as crowded as the massive dance floor, which kept the big band stomping. A haze of cigarette smoke hovered over everyone's heads, making them look like they all had dirty halos in the light from behind the bar.

Lucille, the woman Clem Foxworthy had supposedly been having a serious affair with, was sitting alone at the bar. It was unusual to see a woman on her own in a place like this. But from the way she kept looking over her shoulder, it was obvious she was waiting for someone.

Becky didn't mean to pass judgment on her. When she'd heard that Lucille and Clem were having an affair, she had imagined Lucille to be rather glamorous, with sleepy eyes a man couldn't resist and all her parts in the right places. Sort of like Fanny, who had already surrounded herself with gents who were buying her drinks and lighting her cigarettes.

But Lucille didn't have anyone lighting her cigarette for her. As Becky watched her, she thought Lucille looked sad.

"Wow. She looks like a dishrag hanging on a sink!" Martha shouted back at Becky.

"And she doesn't look like someone who does much baking," Becky replied, making Martha nod. "Why would a girl like her enter a pie contest? Even if it was rigged for her to win, did she really want a blue ribbon that badly?"

If her memory served her right, Becky remembered Mr. Foxworthy as being a slick Willie. He took pride in his appearance. A man didn't have to be a butter-and-egg man to be a member of the Elks. Why, Mr. Dover was just a small-time guy who kept strychnine on his shelf right next to the flour and sugar. But Mr. Foxworthy had had money. Bernice never went without a new coat every winter. And Becky had heard they threw lavish parties in the summer. But the Mackenzies never attended. The reason could have been that the Foxworthys lived in an apartment downtown, or maybe her family wasn't invited for reasons Becky didn't want to entertain. Still, the idea that Mr. Foxworthy was stepping out on his wife with this scrawny young woman came into crystal-clear focus. He was a tramp.

And it was a clearer motive to kill the man than anything else Becky had uncovered so far. It was better than the thought that Mrs. Brower could have done it based on her past behavior—maybe she'd hoped to poison Mrs. Hindergast's pie and ruin her reputation so she could never enter a pie contest again. And it beat the idea that Mr. Dover was so angry with Mr. Foxworthy continually belittling him that he had slipped into a daydream and added that poison without even realizing he'd done it.

Before Becky could say anything to Martha about her conclusion, Vincent No-cent came waltzing into the joint looking as dapper as could be. He was sporting a well-worn suit, and his shoes could have used a shine. But his hair was combed, and Becky could tell he'd had a shave since the last time she had seen him.

He searched the bar, and when he saw Lucille, he smoothed his hair and marched right up to her. She smiled, grateful she wouldn't have to sit at the bar alone any longer, and looked up at him from beneath long lashes. From his body language and the way he took Lucille's hand and admired her, it was obvious to Becky that No-cent was complimenting her dress. Lucille smiled.

As Becky watched, she couldn't help feeling ashamed of herself. Here were two people who might have been behind the eight ball more than once in their lives, yet they'd found each other.

After a few minutes of formality, Lucille asked No-cent a question. He nodded and then reached into his pocket as he looked around nervously. Becky was sure he'd given her a roll of cash that even she found stunning. Lucille quickly took it in her hand and immediately thrust it down the top of her blouse. Then Lucille did something Becky wasn't expecting: she started to cry.

No-cent patted her shoulder and held her hands. They stared at each other for a long minute before Lucille hugged No-cent as if he was a life preserver and she was drowning. Looking the happiest she had all night, Lucille grabbed No-cent by one hand and wiped her tears away with the other. Within seconds, she had gotten down off her stool and was leading No-cent out the door.

"What do you suppose that was all about?" Martha shouted over the music.

"I think it was a payoff," Becky replied.

Even though that was what the whole scene had looked like, there was something in the way Lucille Clementine and Vincent No-cent had acted together that kept her in her seat instead of in hot pursuit. It just didn't feel right. Becky realized that she might be letting the bad guys get away. But what had Clem Foxworthy done to Lucille? She didn't look like a gold digger.

Heck, all Becky had to do was take a gander at her cousin, who was gushing over what were undoubtedly stupid comments by two stiffs lousy with dough, looking for an arm ornament. There was one thing Becky could say about Fanny: she was no chippie and didn't skate around. If a fella wanted to buy her drinks and light her cigarettes, she'd let them. But if they wanted any more than that, they were going to have to prove it in the daylight.

Lucille looked like a pretty girl without a head on her shoulders who had fallen for a line and now regretted it. If that was truly the case, Becky wasn't so sure Lucille hadn't done the world a favor by poisoning Foxworthy.

That isn't very Christian, her conscience said as loudly as the bells at Notre Dame.

"Should we tail them?" Becky asked Martha.

"I don't know, Beck. Do you want to find out that they did it and Judge helped?" Martha asked. "You said you saw him give some money to No-cent. I guess I'm just wondering if it wouldn't be better to let sleeping dogs lie."

Becky tossed back the last of her drink and shook her head. "Let's stay put. The music is good tonight."

"Atta girl." Martha put her arm around Becky and gave her a squeeze.

The rest of the evening was lively. Becky twirled around the floor a couple of times, and each time she did, Stephen Penbroke was her partner. He lifted her off her feet as if she weighed no more than a feather. But even through the jokes Teddy was rattling off and the banter between her and Stephen, Becky held the image of Lucille looking so sad in her mind. There was nothing worse than a broken heart. And it didn't matter where a girl lived, whether it was in a shotgun shack or on a tobacco plantation; love was not a guarantee.

Martha, who had emptied her own flask some time ago, was sending Teddy back to the bar for one more round when Becky leaned over, linked her arm through her friend's, and held her fast.

"So, when were you going to tell me about Adam?" Becky asked.

Martha sobered up quickly. "Oh, Becky. I wanted to tell you. You have to believe me."

"I do, Martha. But what did you think I was going to do? Kill him? Kill myself?" Becky asked.

"Of course not. But how do you tell your best friend any bad news? And what if you didn't believe me? I couldn't bear to have you mad at me, Beck. Not even for a minute," Martha replied. "My hope was that Adam would leave town after a little coaxing from Teddy and the boys. Maybe he'd decide to go on back to Chicago. Then I wouldn't have to tell you. I'd just have to cheer you up."

"You are a peach, Martha. Can you tell me what happened? How you found out?" Becky asked.

"All I know is what Teddy told me. He'd heard *something* through the grapevine." Martha shrugged. "Then he swore me to secrecy and said he was going to handle it. So, truthfully, I don't know any more than you."

"What did Teddy mean by handle it? I don't think he's ever been in a fight in his whole life. He's a gum bumper." Becky chuckled.

"That is true. But he knows people. Look at him." Martha pointed toward the bar, where Teddy was shaking hands and clapping the gents on the back while complimenting the ladies before he started to stroll back to the table with another round of drinks.

"When you say he knows people, you don't think he'd hire a Johnson brother, do you?" Becky gasped.

"I don't know, Becky. All I do know is that when it comes to you, Teddy is the guy you want on your side. Faithful through and through. He adores you," Martha said.

"Hey, what's with the storm cloud? You ladies look like you need to wet the whistle," Teddy said when he finally made it back to the table.

Becky shook off her melancholy just enough to make a few more turns around the dance floor. When it was time to go home, Becky insisted Stephen give Martha and Fanny a lift. She wanted to talk to Teddy alone. From the look on his face, he knew why, and he obliged without argument.

"I don't see why I have to go with you. No offense to either of you, of course." Fanny huffed. "But we do live in the same house."

"It's a long yarn, Fanny. Just get in the car," Martha said, holding the door open for her.

"Don't take me to the front door, Teddy," Becky said once they were on their way. "Take me around to the Old Brick Cemetery entrance. I'll cut through."

"Are you sure? It's a cool night. I wouldn't want you to catch your death of cold."

"I won't." Becky folded her arms and looked at Teddy as he was driving.

He took a deep breath and shook his head.

"The other night at Willie's, the night you didn't come with us, I was at the end of the bar, not far from the door, when I noticed ol' No-cent come strolling in. I was sure there was going to be a row, because he owes about every juice joint in town money. But you can imagine I nearly had kittens when I saw him pay his tab." Teddy shrugged.

Becky thought of the money her father had given No-cent that night at the Elks Club when he didn't know she was there.

"So, I said well done, Vincent. Can I buy you a round? I thought a fella making good on what he owes deserves a reward. But hold onto your hat. You know what he tells me?" Teddy asked, making Becky shake her head. "He tells me he's dried up. Never going to touch a drop of liquor again."

"Wow," Becky said and blinked. Sure, she was happy for No-cent, but this wasn't the story she was looking for. She waited patiently.

"So when I asked him why the sudden about-face, he said it was for a dame. I couldn't think of a better reason. So I shook his hand and had a drink for him. That was when Adam walked in," Teddy said sadly.

Becky watched the anger fall over his face. He didn't look anything like himself. It looked like he'd suddenly gotten his feathers ruffled, and he appeared bigger than usual.

"And?" Becky asked.

"No-cent took one look at Adam, and his whole demeanor changed. He marched right up to him and said, 'You're courting Judge Mackenzie's daughter, ain't ya? That pretty little redheaded gal?' Adam looked at No-cent like he'd been caught cheating at craps."

"Why?" Becky asked.

"No-cent said, 'I saw you with that floozy over at that dive on Maple Street. How could you do that to Judge Mackenzie's daughter?'" Teddy swallowed hard. "I stepped up and asked Adam what No-cent was talking about. Adam hadn't noticed me at first. But as soon as he saw me, I could tell that what No-cent was saying was true. Adam looked at me and shrugged. I couldn't believe it. He shrugged," Teddy replied. "I lost my temper. I was going to kill him,

Beck. Plain and simple. But the boys at the bar slipped between us, and Adam left before I could get my mitts on him."

Becky sat there, looking at Teddy and then focusing on the road ahead. It felt like the trip took a matter of minutes. Just as Teddy finished, they were pulling down the road that led to the cemetery. Becky's mouth had gone dry, and she did feel a shiver across the back of her shoulders.

"Becky, I'm so sorry. I should have told you sooner. I hope you're not mad at your old pal Teddy. But this was sticky, and I didn't know what to do," he said as he stopped the car in front of the rusty old gate.

"I could never be mad at you, Theodore," Becky said, hoping the tears in her eyes were not noticeable in the dark. She kissed Teddy on the cheek. "Martha is a very lucky girl."

"Adam was a lucky guy. He just didn't know how lucky," Teddy said.

Becky waved good-bye and blew Teddy one more kiss before she walked into the cemetery.

It was a lot cooler than Becky had realized. She wrapped her arms around herself and began to walk the well-worn path she'd taken a million times. Peace seemed to have settled over the cemetery. The spirits that Becky usually saw were in their usual places, talking to the loved ones only they saw or giving a cordial greeting to their spiritual neighbors.

The Old Brick Cemetery was on the other side of the Mackenzie plantation but was a quicker route to her front door than going down the road and up the long dirt driveway. Ever since childhood, Becky had been drawn to the place. Her gift of gab with those recently and long since deceased had come in handy when there were no other children for her to play with.

Mr. Wilcox, a kindly old gent who looked like Santa Claus in overalls, was not just one of her first ghostly friends but was a staple at the old cemetery. Whenever Becky walked through, no matter what time of the day or night, he always made an appearance. Tonight was no exception.

"Why the long face, honey?" Mr. Wilcox asked as if Becky was kin. Maybe he didn't know he was passed on. Maybe he did and still wanted to enjoy the beautiful trees and flowers that grew wild in the untended cemetery. Becky didn't know. But kindness radiated from Mr. Wilcox like the smell of tobacco came from her father.

"I got a little bad news is all," Becky replied. "But it ain't no real trouble. How are you?"

Becky sat down on the cobblestone pathway as Mr. Wilcox took a seat on a weathered tombstone and began to tell her about his family. Some of the stories she'd heard before, like those of his wife, who was as pretty as a field in early May, or of his old hound dog that loved to sleep on his porch. She didn't know how long she was there, but she felt better after hearing Mr. Wilcox's stories.

"I sure do enjoy your company, Mr. Wilcox. But I've got to get home," Becky said after a while. "It's getting late."

"You come and see me again, honey, and tell me about your news. Maybe together we'll come up with a solution." Mr. Wilcox smiled kindly, his eyes crinkling up and almost getting swallowed by the wrinkles.

"I will do that," Becky said as she dusted off her dress and walked the rest of the way to her house.

Before she reached the part of the fence where she'd slip through the small iron archway, which was the other entrance, she saw the huge weeping willow she loved to sit beneath on warm, sunny days and draw in her sketchbook. But right now, there was a woman standing there that Becky had never seen before. At first, she thought it was a real person. But as she crept closer, she saw no feet, just the hem of her dress hanging down and disappearing into nothing.

"Good evening," Becky said politely. Her voice cut through the darkness like a sharp knife through a piece of cake.

The woman didn't immediately turn around. Becky just wanted to be polite, since this was not really her place of residence. It was the home of the spirits buried here. But since she came so regularly, she wanted to be friendly nonetheless.

"I did it," the woman whispered. Her voice was soft and sad.

"I beg your pardon?" Becky asked.

"I did it. I killed him. But it was only because I loved him so much. Do you know how it feels to love someone that much?" The woman sobbed.

"I...don't know..." Becky stuttered. Those were not the words she'd expected to hear in response to her greeting. But before she could continue on her way, the spirit turned around. Her dress was stained with dark patches, her hands were covered with blood, and her face looked like that of a ghastly, forever-doomed Lucille Clementine.

With a start, Becky sat up straight in bed. She stared ahead, looking around and letting the memory of her dream sift away as her heart calmed at the sight of the familiar arrangement of her room.

"What in the world?"

Becky rubbed her hand over her face. She'd made it home hours ago and had come into the house through the front door. There was no woman underneath the weeping willow. No woman who looked like Lucille Clementine had confessed to murder. But what did it mean? Becky didn't know.

She lay back down and pulled her quilt up to her chin, and although she tried, she couldn't fall back to sleep.

CHAPTER NINETEEN

$\mathcal{F}$anny sashayed from one end of the parlor to the other, where Becky was sitting quietly with her sketchbook in one hand and a pencil in the other.

"I don't care if you tag along or not. I'm just telling you that Stephen promised to come back this evening to take us to the fireworks show tonight." Fanny clicked her tongue as she looked at her reflection in a small mirror on the wall. "To be honest, you've been such a grump lately that I don't think it would be a good idea for you to come."

"You're just saying that because you want Stephen all to yourself," Becky said, making her hands into claws and scratching out at Fanny like a cat.

"No, I'm saying it because it's true. My goodness, they would have run you out of every party in all of France with your grumpy disposition. It's embarrassing." Fanny huffed as she walked to the love seat and took a seat.

"Why are you in here? Just to drive me batty?" Becky asked.

"I want to know what you and Teddy talked about last night. That was a lot of hoopla so he could take you home by himself. There's got to be something going on," Fanny said, her eyes twinkling with delight as she hoped to hear some gossip.

"Well, Fanny, you are going to hear about it sooner or later," Becky replied. She took a deep breath and looked at the drawing she was working on before looking back at Fanny. "Adam and I are on the outs."

Fanny gasped. She made no attempt to hide her pleasure in the situation. "Why?" Her voice had not a drop of compassion in it.

"What difference does it make?" Becky asked.

"What are you going to do?" Fanny prodded.

"Nothing. If he wants to step out, I can't stop him. But I won't let him keep doing it," Becky replied. She looked at her cousin, who was calculating the proper amount of time it would require before she could make a move on Adam herself.

"That is one tall, cool glass of water," Fanny needled. "That's really too bad. But what do you expect?"

"What?"

"I don't mean to add salt to the wound, Rebecca," Fanny said.

"Of course not," Becky muttered under her breath.

"But you just don't know how to handle the opposite sex. Now, when I was in Paris, I learned by observing the very fine art of luring and keeping a fellow interested. It's actually quite an art form. It's really rather unfair that women are not taught to use their womanly wiles to keep a man. You took him for granted. No man likes that." Fanny proceeded to inspect her nails.

"Well, that certainly explains all the suitors banging down our front door. Oh wait," Becky said.

There was no doubt that in a plain, old-fashioned beauty contest, Fanny would win. She was gorgeous and knew it. But Fanny never gave her own looks a second thought. No one ever turned her down for a dance at any speakeasy, and to her, that said a lot more than having a couple good-looking but dumb apes leering at her.

"I don't invite any suitors to the house because this isn't my house. I believe it would break Aunt Kitty's heart if the only fellas to come calling were for me," Fanny said as she stood up. "Now, I'd love to sit here and chat with you about it, but I have to go pick out what I'm going to wear tonight for the fireworks."

Becky watched as Fanny sashayed out of the room, her skirt swishing back and forth like the waves of an ocean.

"Of all the members of the house to be scarce or leave town, why couldn't it have been Fanny?" Becky muttered.

She looked down at her sketch and felt a strange pluck in the middle of her chest. It was a drawing of Lucille Clementine but not the woman sitting alone at the bar at Racy Jack's. It was a specter under the willow tree that Becky had dreamt of. Her sunken eyes stared back at Becky as if she were still in the cemetery and being told that the ghost had "killed him because she loved him." What did it mean? She certainly couldn't prove to the police Lucille did it based on a nightmare.

Without giving her drawing or her dream

another thought, Becky went upstairs to her room to take a nap. She hadn't decided if she was going to go along with Stephen or not, especially since she wasn't sure how true his invitation to the fireworks was. Perhaps he just wanted to go with Fanny. That would suit Becky just fine.

But after dinner, when the sun was starting to set, Becky retreated to the front porch swing with a tall, cool mint julep and bare feet. It was just a matter of a quarter of an hour of being relaxed before the shiny flivver with the most handsome blond driver Becky had ever seen pulled up in front of the house.

"Now, you look like you're ready to see some fireworks," Stephen said with a sly grin.

"Your date will be down in a minute," Becky smirked.

"What are you talking about?"

"Fanny made it perfectly clear that she was your date for the evening. I don't feel like going out," Becky replied as she pushed herself slowly on the porch swing.

"Oh, now that ain't true. Teddy told me about your breakup with Adam, and I am specifically here to cheer you up. The last thing a girl should do when she's got a broken heart is to stay home alone," Stephen said as he marched up the steps. "Now, you can either come peacefully, or I'll just have to scoop you up and carry you to the car."

"That would be kidnapping, and my daddy just won't allow it."

"Where is Judge? I'd certainly like to give him a hearty handshake and tell him I'm here to court his daughter like a proper Southern gentleman." Stephen let himself into the house just as Moxley was coming through the parlor.

"Good evening, Mr. Penbroke," Moxley said with a smile.

"Hello, Moxley. Can you point me in the direction of Mr. Mackenzie?" Stephen asked after shaking Moxley's hand.

"I'm sorry, but Mr. Mackenzie is out for the evening," Moxley replied rather awkwardly.

Stephen didn't notice. Instead, he shrugged and wished Moxley a good night before reappearing on the porch. "Now I can't leave you here. Your daddy isn't home. It's bad luck to stay alone on a night when there's a firework display scheduled. Now get your shoes on, girl, and get in my car. Let's go!"

Just then, Fanny appeared and nearly toppled Stephen as she ran into his arms.

"Oh, it's just so sweet of you to drive to the fireworks. It has been sheer torture waiting all day for this excursion," Fanny said while sweetly batting her lashes and flipping her blond hair over her shoulder. "Becky says she doesn't feel like going, so it looks like it's just you and I."

"Becky's coming with, aren't you, Beck?" Stephen grinned at her. "Pretty please with a cherry on top?"

Becky hated that Stephen was so cute, especially when all she really wanted to do was wallow in her misery over her mother not being there when she needed her and over Adam making her need her mother. She didn't know if she was more upset or plain aggravated.

"Fine. Do I need to change my clothes?" Becky asked as she stood from the swing. She was wearing a simple cotton dress with a wide collar. It was a real change from the violet dress she'd been wearing the night before that had made her look like she just stepped off the movie screen.

"No one cares how you look, Becky," Fanny replied as she walked toward Stephen's car. "I doubt anyone will even pay any attention."

"You look swell. Just grab a pair of shoes, and we're off," Stephen said.

Becky wasn't going to argue with Fanny, who had already climbed into the front seat to make sure she was within pawing distance.

Within minutes, they were well on their way. It was the final night of the Savannah Dog Days and Firecracker Festival. When they reached the fairgrounds, where the fireworks display would be in full view, it appeared that all of Savannah was in attendance.

"I think we have to go through the fair to the open ground where the fireworks will be," Becky said. "I don't know. I don't think this was a very good idea."

"Why not?" Stephen asked. "Why, I wouldn't be surprised if we ran into Martha and Teddy here. And probably half a dozen other people you know. This might be hard to believe, Rebecca, but you are well liked in these parts. Adam was a fool."

The last thing Becky wanted was to hear his name. She hated that as she walked through the festivities, she couldn't help but keep her eyes peeled for the tall, broad-shouldered, dark-haired, two-timing dog who, up until a couple days ago, had been the love of her life. He still was. She hated to say it, but she couldn't just turn off her feelings.

But Becky knew one thing: once a cheater, always a cheater. She'd seen it firsthand with lots of the flappers she knew from the clubs. Pretty girls with street smarts. But when it came to love, they let the same sheiks use the same lines over and over, making them look bad and feel worse. Becky was heartbroken, but she wasn't stupid. No matter how much it was going to hurt, she'd eventually have to confront Adam. And then she'd turn her back on him. The fact that Teddy had been ready to fight for her honor made her want to cry. He was a good egg.

"How about some cotton candy? It's the last night of the fair. You won't get any for another year," Stephen offered.

"That sounds swell." Becky played the good sport.

"Becky, I do believe that Nat Phine is over there, conversing with that strong man." Fanny pointed to a big blue tent with a picture of a man in a leopard skin flexing his muscles painted on the side and the actual man standing in front of it.

Next to him, sure enough, was Nat. She was almost as much of a spectacle as he was with her pretty dress, which couldn't help but accentuate what she had in abundance.

"Come on. Let's go say hello," Becky said.

"My goodness, Rebecca," Fanny said. "It's bad enough everyone knows you are friends with that Gypsy woman, but now you want to flaunt your bizarre taste in associates with this woman? You can go ahead and ruin your reputation. I will do nothing of the sort."

"Suit yourself. Tell Stephen I'll be back in a jiffy." Becky smoothed out her dress and suddenly wished she'd dressed a little better for the occasion. But that wasn't enough to stop her.

As she approached, she heard Nat's loud laugh and saw the glistening gems of different colors on her fingers. Not to mention her bright-red hair. As soon as Nat glanced in Becky's direction, a look of recognition lit up her face, and she laughed even louder.

"Becky! Now isn't this a happy coincidence." She waved.

"Hi, Nat. You are the last person I thought I'd run into here," Becky said.

"Oh, you know what they say. The criminal always returns to the scene of the crime. So I've got my eyes peeled." She ran her fingers through the strings of pearls around her neck as she laughed. "Becky Mackenzie, I'd like you to meet Lorenzo, the strongest man on Earth."

"Miss Mackenzie."

Lorenzo was taller than Adam, who reached a height of at least six feet, and wore a black-and-white–striped leotard with a leopard-printed loincloth. His arms and legs bulged with muscles, and his head was as smooth as an egg. He had blue eyes that twinkled playfully. He extended his giant hand toward Becky, who graciously shook it. He was as gentle as a lamb.

"It's a pleasure to meet you, Lorenzo." Becky smiled and blinked in awe.

Lorenzo stood back and began flexing his muscles for the crowd of people, who marveled as they walked by.

"I'm going to tell you something, Becky," Nat began. "I'd like to pay your mama a visit, because of all the people in this town, she has raised you right. Do you know that you are the only person to come and pay me a visit who wasn't wearing copper buttons or had her nose in a snit over my buying that old colonial? And I swear, half the town thinks I killed that Foxworthy fellow."

"I'm so sorry, Nat. I do hope that doesn't make you want to leave town," Becky worried.

"Do I look like I could kill someone?" She held up her delicate hands with her glistening rings and red polish.

"Not to me," Becky replied.

"But she is a thief!" Lorenzo yelled. "She's stolen

my heart!" Then he lifted a huge dumbbell that had the number "200" painted on its surface.

Nat roared with laughter and waved to Lorenzo like she was shooing a fly.

"Are you staying for the fireworks? It would be delightful if you'd sit with us," Becky asked.

"Who is us?" Nat blinked.

"My dear friend Stephen Penbroke, and you remember my cousin Fanny," Becky replied.

"She's the one who went to Paris?" Nat asked as if she were trying to stifle a laugh. Becky nodded and shrugged. "Well, normally, I'd say yes. I'd just love to. But I've got an engagement that I can't break. It's sort of a business deal, and I just can't be late or bring anyone with. My partner gets a little jumpy."

"Oh, I see." Becky was obviously disappointed.

"I didn't know that the people of Savannah were so thirsty," Nat said with a wink.

Becky understood completely. She was a rum runner. Becky didn't know if she was shocked or if she just admired Nat all the more. And she couldn't help but wonder where Nat kept her flasks, since her dress left very little wiggle room.

"I understand." Becky smiled.

"But I want you and your friends to come see me sometime. The ice is always cold, and the music is always hot." Nat shimmied, making several passing fellows trip over themselves. Nat laughed out loud, and her laugh was as contagious as a yawn, making Becky giggle too.

"That sounds great, Nat. Oh, and do you want to get your fortune told?" Becky asked.

"What?"

"My dear friend Madame Cecelia is the fortune-teller in the tent near the scene of the crime. If you are keeping your eyes peeled, stop in and tell her I sent you," Becky said as she waved.

"I think I'll just do that, honey." Nat waved before turning back to Lorenzo. He swooped up to her, and they began talking again.

Becky was amazed at Natalie Phine. She'd seen rum runners around town and knew a couple of girls who made their living doing that to small-time joints and penny-ante thugs. But from the looks of things, Nat was earning herself a pretty penny and lots of them to boot. What was the harm? Even Mrs. Merriweather took a snort now and again. Becky was sure of it. The thought of that old biddy high as a kite was a sight Becky would have paid money to see.

As Becky walked back to where she'd left Fanny, she looked around and didn't see her. Oh, it would be just like Fanny to pull Stephen aside to have him all to herself. Not that Becky cared about that. The last thing she wanted at the moment was to replace Adam with a blond-haired, blue-eyed proxy. It was just too soon. Heck, Becky hadn't even spoken to Adam yet. For all he knew, she could have been in the dark about the whole sordid affair. But only an ultra-maroon would think Teddy wouldn't have spilled the beans.

Becky wandered through the fair, watching everyone laughing and really having a gay time. She didn't know what was wrong with her. She was supposed to be sad—tearful even—to have found out about Adam, but something inside her just wouldn't budge. With her mother gone and her father out somewhere, she was all messed up.

Just then, high overhead and slightly off in the distance, a huge explosion of white covered the sky. The fireworks had started. Quickly, Becky hurried in the direction of the field behind the fair, where the display was going off. She slipped between people, hearing nothing but laughter and the lively music that came from the rides. Barkers' words jumbled together as they enticed the crowd to try their luck at one of the games in order to win a Kewpie doll.

Cigarette smoke and the scent of popcorn mingled in the cool air. The energy of the fairgrounds was so thick it could be cut with a knife. Everyone was enjoying themselves, getting in one last ride on the merry-go-round or stealing one more kiss at the top of the Ferris wheel. The fact that Becky was suddenly alone in this crowd was nice, and she wished she had come to the fair by herself earlier in the week to roam around and see the lights and the rides and not be noticed by anyone. Instead of being bogged down by all the issues going on in her home, she should have sought refuge in the assembly of the good people of Savannah. The whole scene cleared Becky's head.

As she was about to go buy a bag of peanuts to devour herself, she saw Adam. And he saw her.

CHAPTER TWENTY

*F*or a minute, she just stood there, unsure what to do. Should she wave? Should she walk away? Should she make a scene? As it turned out, she did none of these things and instead just smiled wearily and shrugged.

Adam looked at her like a man on a desert island spotting a ship sailing by. With great long strides, he hurried up to her.

"Becky. I've been looking all over for you." He huffed.

"I'm not hard to find," she replied. "I sleep in the same bed every night. But maybe that's an old-fashioned concept to you." It was a petty comment, but she couldn't stop herself.

"It's not anything like that. Becky, it was just a kiss. Please let me explain."

"So, it's true? What Teddy told me is true?" Becky stood still and stared up at Adam, who she was sure was starting to sweat.

"Kind of. Becky, I don't know what happened. Can we please just go somewhere quiet to talk? Maybe you can help me..." He stopped short of what he was saying. His cheeks went red. His eyes darted around from one end of the fair to the other.

"Help you? You know, *I've* had a rough week. *I* needed help. I *needed* a shoulder to lean on. Now I know why I didn't see you."

Becky couldn't bear to listen to any excuse Adam might have had. She shook her head and began to stomp off toward the field, where the fireworks display had begun. Although it wasn't yet fall, the evening had chased the heavy heat of the summer nights away with a cool breeze.

"I didn't know what to say," Adam said. "Then I ran into Teddy, and things went crazy. How could I tell you when I knew that he'd already given you his side of the story?"

"So, what Teddy told me wasn't true? He said he heard it from No-cent," Becky snapped. "That No-cent confronted you, and Teddy was ready to knock your block off after hearing it. Was that not true? Did Teddy lie?"

"No," Adam muttered.

Becky stared at him as if he was a stranger. He looked different. He was still tall and strong and handsome. But the desire was gone. Not just the desire to feel his arms around her as they danced but the desire to know his ideas and thoughts, to understand him, to care for him—all the important things that would remain when age took everything else.

Where was Stephen when she needed him? Heck, she would have been thankful for Fanny to show up. The idea of being alone with Adam made her sick to her stomach, because she didn't know what to do. Should she listen to him? Or was it just a flimflam, an effort to fool her into thinking it was somehow her fault or no one's fault? Like Clem Foxworthy, who'd had a beautiful wife, it wasn't about having a good woman; it was about having as many women as possible.

Becky had had issues with Adam twirling around the dance floor with a few shebas with questionable motives. But he'd reassured her, told her she had nothing to worry about and that he only had eyes for her. She had believed him. She had trusted him.

All of these thoughts were racing through her

mind, but she couldn't focus on anything. The sound of the fair was fading a little as she realized she was off from the crowd with Adam at her side.

"It's quiet here," Becky said as she folded her arms over her chest and avoided Adam's eyes by looking into the darkness. Where was Stephen? Wasn't he looking for her?

"I didn't plan for anything to happen," Adam said. "I just went out with the guys from work, and there she was."

Becky felt sick to her stomach. After all she'd gone through to get her family to accept him, and Kitty had been right all along. A Northerner couldn't be trusted.

"Who was it?" Becky asked.

"You don't know her. She's new in town and…"

"And just needed some kind soul to show her around. How much did you drop on her? Because that sounds like a swindle if I ever heard one," Becky said, doing everything within her power to hold back her tears.

She pinched her arm until she was sure there would be a bruise in the morning. She bit the inside of her lip almost to bleeding. She even held her breath, hoping Adam wouldn't notice her cheeks go red as they stood in the dark shadows.

"It didn't mean anything, Becky," Adam said. "I just lost my head. I was at the Calico Cat. The moonshine was enough to strip the paint off the side of a barn. It was just a kiss. It wasn't anything serious and didn't mean anything."

"It didn't mean anything?" Becky asked.

"Not a thing." He shook his head and took a step closer to Becky. "Not at all. It was a mistake. The biggest mistake I ever made," he said.

"Does she know that?" Becky asked coolly.

Adam took half a step back like he'd been slapped. "What difference does that make?"

Becky couldn't believe her ears. For a second, she wondered if she wasn't having one of those horrible hallucinations again in which people she loved called her names and said the cruelest things to her. She pinched herself so hard she winced. Nope. This wasn't a hallucination. This was real. The man she'd thought she loved, who she'd invited into her family home, was admitting to her that he'd used a woman for a few moments or maybe a half an hour or maybe even an hour or two.

None of that mattered. What mattered was that not only didn't he take Becky's feelings into consideration, he didn't even take this other woman's feelings into consideration. What kind of man did that?

The kind of man that got poisoned at a blueberry pie–tasting contest, that was what kind of man.

"I appreciate you coming clean, Adam," Becky said. She turned to go back into the fair and find herself that bag of roasted peanuts to eat by herself.

"Wait." Adam grabbed Becky's hand, which she tore away from him as if he had leprosy. "I told you it didn't mean anything. Becky, if I could undo what happened, I would. I just got caught up in a moment, and I swear it won't ever happen again."

Just as Becky was about to start arguing, she saw No-cent slipping past the ticket booth and heading toward a small cluster of trees. She couldn't let him get away.

"Becky? Are you listening to me?" Adam huffed.

"Yes, I heard every word," she said, watching No-cent. Becky knew that if Adam saw him, he'd probably want to do a tap dance on his face for letting the cat out of the bag. But Becky wanted to talk to No-cent, not just because he knew about Adam but because of what she had seen between him and Lucille at Racy Jack's.

"Well?"

"Well what?" Becky snapped.

"Am I forgiven or what? It isn't like I robbed a

bank. I kissed another girl. You dance with every suit that walks into a place, and I don't say anything," Adam whined.

Becky looked at Adam and narrowed her eyes just as every tear that had been on the verge of rolling down her cheeks instantly dried up.

"No. You are not forgiven," Becky hissed. She hurried off after No-cent, leaving Adam standing there by himself.

She knew that it would only be a matter of time before the reality of the situation and the damage that had been caused to her heart would sink in. But at this moment, she was hurrying past tents and games and food vendors to catch up with No-cent.

It looked as if he was wearing the same suit he had worn the previous evening. Becky didn't care. She just wanted to talk to him for a second. If he knew that Lucille had killed Foxworthy, Becky wasn't going to say anything to anyone. She'd clam up and take the information to the grave. She wanted to know what he had to do with her father. She wasn't going to ask about Lucille or the pie contest. If Lucille had poisoned her pie and Foxworthy ate it and croaked, well, that was going to be a job for the police. Becky wasn't squealing.

Finally, she saw him take a right through two striped tents. When she passed between the heavy, dusty material that composed the tents, she stopped short as No-cent suddenly appeared in front of her and cut her off.

"Hey! What gives?" he snapped.

"Vincent. I'm Becky Mackenzie. Judge Mackenzie's daughter," she said after swallowing hard and trying to catch her breath.

Vincent No-cent leaned back, pulled a pack of matches from his pocket, struck one, and held it up to see her face. She saw a smile cross his face before he shook the match out.

"That you are. Miss Mackenzie, what are you doing following me behind these tents?" he asked, his voice soft and curious.

"I'm sorry, Vincent. I need to ask you something," Becky said.

The lights from the bumper car ride bounced off the dingy white canvas of the tent and gave her just enough light to see Vincent's face clearly for the first time. He was thin and lanky and not all that easy to look at. His teeth were crooked, with a space between the top two so big a flivver could park there. His hair was short and looked as if he'd cut it himself. But still, there was the quiet dignity of a man who'd changed.

"I don't know if I like the sound of this," Vincent muttered.

"Vincent, just after Clem Foxworthy died, I saw my father give you money. He said you'd done something. What did you do?" Becky asked quietly.

Vincent rubbed the back of his neck with one hand while he thrust the other deep into his pants pocket. "Miss Mackenzie, I do hope you won't repeat this. I know that my reputation was not a stellar one. And I know that you and many others referred to me by nickname."

Becky blushed and felt like a real heel.

"No-cent. The name fit. Is that right?" He looked at Becky intensely. "It's all right, Miss Mackenzie. I spent every nickel I had on hooch. It clung to me like those burrs that grow in the summer around dead wood and fallen trees. You know the kind I mean. They just won't let go till you rip them off, piercing your skin and ruining your clothes in the process."

"I know those," Becky replied.

"Your father helped me get on the wagon," Vincent said.

"I had no idea," Becky replied.

"That is how your father operates. I don't think I've ever known a finer man. I'll admit when your daddy first came across me, I was in bad shape." Vincent shook his head and rubbed his neck again. "I'd stumbled into his tobacco field and passed out. I was hung out to dry. So inebriated was I that I didn't even hear the tractor coming."

"The tractor?" Becky wondered what Vincent was talking about. Daddy hadn't needed to use the tractor on the field for quite some time and wouldn't be turning over the dirt until spring of next year. Perhaps Vincent's mind had the times confused. But if there was any pickling of his brain, Becky wasn't going to point it out and dispute his statement.

"Yes'm," Vincent said confidently. "Had your daddy not been at the helm of that machine, I don't think I would have survived. No one would have seen me until it was too late. But it was no wonder he spotted me. Since then, I watched your daddy as he tended his fields of tobacco, and he knows every inch of land. He saw me, all right. He saw me in my worst, most pathetic state. After a few dunks in a barrel of cold water, I was sobered up. Your daddy made me an offer."

Becky could hardly believe what she was hearing. She'd known her father was a good man. To her, the sun rose and set on him. But she had no idea he'd gone out and done the Lord's work like this. How could he have been with Bernice Foxworthy and still reached down to help one of the lowliest of the low?

"He put me to work on his new field. I couldn't tell you when the last time was that I used my muscles like that. After the first day, I was so tired I didn't have the strength to even crawl to the nearest juice joint. The next day, I was so sore it was the same story. Oh, I wanted a drink so bad, you just can't imagine. But your daddy didn't give up on me," Vincent continued. He pulled a cigarette and a book of matches from his pocket. With the cigarette in his mouth, he started to walk toward the edge of the trees.

"It wasn't much, but he let me sleep in the shed at the Elks Club. He paid me for the work I done. Then he asked me the question that changed my life," Vincent said. Becky couldn't tell for sure, but she thought Vincent was crying.

"What was that?" she asked.

"He asked me what I wanted to do with my life," Vincent replied. In the soft glow of the lights, which were farther off now as they got closer to the trees, Becky saw Vincent's face crinkle with a smile.

"What did you tell him?"

"I said I wanted to go and live off the land in a place that had snow. And I wanted my girl to come with me," Vincent replied as he stood a little taller at the mention of a girl.

"Was that girl Lucille Clementine?" Becky asked. Her heart started to race. She realized that she'd absently followed Vincent to a secluded part of the field, away from the main activities and crowd.

"That she was. I loved her since the day I first set eyes on her," Vincent said, putting the cigarette in his mouth but not lighting it.

"Well, I think that's wonderful," Becky replied.

"It's all right, Miss Mackenzie. I know what you're thinking. Lucille isn't one of those high-society gals. She's got a reputation. I don't begrudge the girl that. What bothered me is the way that Clem Foxworthy got her that reputation."

Becky's breath hitched in her throat. "What do you mean?"

"Lucille was in love with him. And he let her believe he was going to take her away from Savannah. I swear, that low-down dog enjoyed feeding her a line and watching her tie herself up in it," Vincent hissed. "The last straw came on the day of the pie contest."

This was it. Becky was sure that Vincent was

going to confess to slipping poison into one of the pies, or that Lucille had decided to poison Foxworthy and Vincent knew it. As much as she wanted to know the truth, there was part of her that didn't want to hear it.

Even if Foxworthy deserved it—and from the sound of it, he did—Becky thought Vincent and Lucille had encountered enough in this town. If she didn't know they murdered him, she'd never have to carry their secret.

"Vincent, I don't blame you and Lucille for doing what you did. But murder is murder, and I can't…"

Vincent pulled the cigarette he hadn't lit from his mouth and chuckled. "Murder? Do you think Lucille and I killed him?" he asked.

"Didn't you?"

"Why, no, Miss Mackenzie. Lucille entered the pie contest at the last minute to make ol' Clem nervous. She said she wanted to clear her conscience before she started a new life, and he was terrified that had to do with squealing to his wife, who was no dummy and, sure as I'm standing here, knew her ol' husband's stepping out often." Vincent chuckled.

"But I saw you that day. You slipped out of the tent Clem Foxworthy was in, and you went to the pond and threw something in. It was a bottle or something," Becky replied as if she were upset that Vincent and Lucille hadn't committed murder. She decided then and there that she needed a new hobby.

"That was my flask, Miss Mackenzie. It was full to the brim. I threw that thing away so I'd never see it again. I haven't had a drop to drink for over six months. And I don't plan on going back. Not now. Now that Lucille is free from Foxworthy's spell and wants to come with me." His back straightened, and his shoulders squared as he said these words.

"I am embarrassed, Vincent. And I'm sorry. It's just that when I saw you with my father and he was giving you money and telling you to leave town, I didn't know what else to think." Becky felt awful. And she didn't think she could have been more wrong about two people had she tried.

"Ha! Your daddy gave me my last bit of pay for my work on his field and a bonus of sorts. But if I was truly going to start over with a new life, I wanted no reason to ever come back to Savannah. I went around town and paid my debts." Vincent clicked his tongue. "Oh, goodness. Miss Mackenzie, I saw that fella you hang on and…"

"I heard." Becky stopped him before he could say Adam had been stepping out on her.

"I had to put the finger on him. After all your

daddy did for me and the times I heard him jabbering on about you, I knew exactly who you were. I'd seen you at half the roadhouses I owed money to." Vincent chuckled again. "If you were kin to Judge MacKenzie, I knew you were good stock. I felt it was my duty to step in."

"I do appreciate it, Vincent," Becky said. She was almost moved to tears by his devotion to her family.

"I lost my temper that night I saw him. See, a fella like him don't have to worry about his reputation. Just like Foxworthy, he'd look like a big shot. Meanwhile, you'd look like a chump. I'm sorry, Miss Mackenzie. But out of respect for your father, I had to say something." Vincent put the cigarette between his lips but still didn't light it. Becky wondered if he was trying to give up ciggies too.

Just then, the sky lit up with another brilliant display of fireworks. Becky and Vincent both looked up. The loud pops and crackles, along with the gasps from the crowd that had filled the field, drowned out the sounds of the fair rides and cheers. The sky lit up in bold colors of red, blue, green, and white. It was something beautiful that, for the moment, distracted Becky from the heartache over Adam.

"I'm sorry I had to learn about it the way I did. But I thank you for protecting my name, for whatever it's worth." She chuckled. "And now it's my turn to confess something. I was sure that Lucille had something to do with Foxworthy's death. She had the motive. And when I saw you and her together, it made perfect sense."

"Ha! No, ma'am. We didn't kill Foxworthy. I would have liked to punch him in the face. There is no doubt about that. But we didn't kill him. But as sure as I'm standing here, Miss Mackenzie, I know who did," Vincent whispered.

"My goodness, Vincent. Who?" Becky whispered back.

"Someone you'd never guess." He struck the match and raised it to the cigarette in his mouth.

Just then, there was a loud pop. Vincent crumpled to the ground.

"Vincent? Vincent, what is it? Are you o..." Becky stopped.

She crouched next to him, taking his hand in hers. Her breath was punched out of her lungs. Vincent's legs had appeared to just give out on him. He folded over onto himself, only to fall flat on his face. Dead. A dark spot spread out on the back of his jacket. He'd been shot.

The lights from the fireworks were no longer lovely. Instead, they gave everything a menacing, eerie glow as they flashed then slowly faded. They made the shadows seem all that much darker, hiding things even more sinister than Becky had ever imagined.

Someone had been watching them this whole time. They were just waiting in the shadows. Becky looked around nervously. Like a rabbit searching for the movement of a predator out of the corner of her eyes, she didn't dare move.

Every sound made the hairs on her neck stand up. Every branch that waved made her squint into the darkness, seeking the silhouette of an approaching person. The smell of blood, sweet and coppery, filled her nostrils and saturated her taste buds as poor Vincent continued to bleed, even though he was already deceased.

Becky couldn't wait there any longer. Something told her that whoever had pulled the trigger was inching closer and closer to her. It felt as if she was lifting a ton of bricks as she pushed herself to her feet and took off running toward the field and the lights of the fair.

Behind her was the sound of pounding footsteps. Whoever had killed Vincent was after her. And from the sound of it, they were a lot bigger than Becky.

"Help! He...!"

"Stop that shouting, gal!"

Becky heard a male voice behind her and then felt one strong hand grab her by the arm while the hard muzzle of a gun was pressed into her side. "You just settle down and walk."

CHAPTER TWENTY-ONE

The fireworks continued overhead, making Becky feel as if she was in a bizarre, scary dream as the colors flashed and faded, flashed and faded along the ground and across the upturned faces of the spectators. She didn't know who was guiding her past the field, but Becky tried to scan the crowd and find Stephen. Where could he have gone? Where was Fanny?

As if by Divine intervention, Becky saw Fanny kneeling on what looked like Stephen's jacket, pointing up to the sky and smiling happily. Fanny had no idea that Becky was being led right past her by a man she didn't even know.

"Where are we going?" Becky asked.

"Shut your pie hole and walk," the man snarled. "You'll see soon enough."

Stephen was on the other side of Fanny, and although Becky was sure that when he looked over his shoulder, he was searching for her, she was annoyed that he was looking in the wrong direction. No one in the entire crowd noticed her. They were too busy looking up.

Surprisingly, the man led her right into the fair, which was still packed full of people. Becky tried to think of what to do. Should she break free and run? Should she fall to the ground and attract all sorts of attention to herself? Just as she was about to make a decision, she felt the hot breath of her captor on her neck.

"If you think of doing anything stupid, I want you to know that I know where your father has been spending his time, and I know what relative your mother is visiting. So if you get away, you'll be an orphan," he hissed.

Becky felt her knees go weak. Who was this monster pushing her along? He manipulated her through the crowd, never once loosening his grip on her arm, making it throb. Not a single person seemed to see her. She was just another fair attendee looking for one more ride on the bumper cars or a chance to snag the golden ring. Nothing more. She certainly wasn't a woman who had a gun pressed into her side.

As she was being muscled through the crowd, they passed Madame Cecelia's fortune-telling tent. Becky looked inside and saw Ophelia reading someone's tarot cards. Madame Cecelia was nowhere to be seen. Lorenzo, who was still flexing his muscles and smiling at the crowd, winked at Becky as she passed, but she couldn't do anything to get herself some help.

"You're doing just fine. You keep walking, and the hard part will be over. You do what we say, and you'll be back at home in your own bed within the next couple days," her captor said.

"Couple days? Where are you taking me?" Becky muttered back, almost talking over her shoulder.

"You don't ask the questions here. Just keep walking," he grumbled as they got closer and closer to the entrance of the fair. Becky knew if she didn't make a move, she would disappear into that dark field and might never be seen again.

Just then, she saw Adam. He was pacing back and forth in front of a ticket booth and a cotton candy vendor. But as she passed him, he turned in the opposite direction, missing her completely.

She was led through the huge field, weaving in and out among the cars, which had been parked in random patterns as people showed up after visiting the nearest speakeasy or after taking a couple snorts from their own flasks. It looked like a traffic jam. The farther they walked, the softer the sounds of the fair became, as if Becky was being put into a box in which all sense of hearing was being muffled and her sense of sight was being diminished. The only thing she was able to do was feel the hard point of the gun still in her side. She could smell the man's skin and was sure he hadn't had a wash in a very long time but tried to cover his stench with cologne. The combination of the two dueling scents was nauseating until Becky realized she'd smelled it before.

At first, she thought about the gents she cut the rug with at Racy Jack's and was sure she had to have encountered this aroma there. But it didn't ring a bell. Surely, she would have remembered who she danced with. She would have certainly made a comment to Martha, but there was nothing in her recollection that put her and her smelly four-flusher together. Who was this man, and how did he know her?

"Psst! Psst!"

Becky looked to the left and nearly tripped over her own feet.

"Talbot!" Mrs. Gilmore hissed. "What took you so long?"

"Talbot?" Becky muttered. Now she remembered exactly where she'd smelled the strong cologne and where she'd heard the name. The man was Mrs. Gilmore's sneaky tenant, who smelled of Aqua Velva.

"Don't act so innocent, Lady Jane," Mrs. Gilmore scolded. "Did you really think I didn't know exactly what you were up to?"

"Mrs. Gilmore, what are you talking about?" Becky huffed.

"Get her in the car. Because you dillydallied, we're stuck behind these jalopies and have to wait." Mrs. Gilmore grunted. "I saw our friend on the way in. She'll be back, and we can drop the goods then hopefully get out of here."

Becky wasn't sure how long they waited in Mrs. Gilmore's car. The smell of Mr. Talbot's Aqua Velva and body odor was enough to make Becky feel light-headed. Surely, Stephen and Fanny had to know there was something wrong. Would they think to come out here looking for her? Probably not at the moment, because the fireworks display was still going on just a short distance beyond the fair. Becky watched the lights and tried to think of what to do. But she had a gun to her side. Talbot had made no indication his hand was even tired.

"Why are you doing this, Mrs. Gilmore?" Becky asked.

"You and that Vincent thought you could put the squeeze on me. Like I haven't dealt with people like you before. Think you can blackmail me, do you?" Mrs. Gilmore was no longer the sweet old lady who had invited Becky into her kitchen. "I didn't get where I am by being a fool."

"Get where you are? The owner of a house who rents out her rooms?" Becky asked.

"Very funny. Was it you who came up with the idea to try and blackmail me, or was it your rummy friend, the late Mr. Vincent? Something in my gut told me I shouldn't have rented him a room."

"Vincent was your tenant?" Becky gasped.

"Of course he was my tenant. Don't play stupid. He was there the day you stopped by, lurking around upstairs, quiet as a church mouse, listening while you pulled information out of me. Your father had gotten him the room after he'd stopped drinking. I thought he would have been a valuable tenant for my image. He was cleaning up his act. At least that's what I thought," Mrs. Gilmore said then spat through her open window. "Turned out he knew what I'd done. I don't know how he figured it out. I guess I'll never know. But he figured it out, all right, and thought I should pay him to keep his mouth shut."

"He was leaving town. He and Lucille Clementine were leaving together. He wasn't going to rat on anyone," Becky said. Her heart went out to Lucille, who was probably waiting for Vincent at this very moment.

"Dummy up!" hissed Talbot. "Here she comes."

Becky followed their gazes and saw Natalie Phine walking their way, clinging to the arm of a big palooka Becky had never seen before. He let go of Nat's arm and went to a sleek car with no roof while she made her way to Mrs. Gilmore, her hips swishing back and forth as if she was walking on the deck of a boat in rough waters.

"Fancy meeting you here. I'll say one thing about you Georgians: you are punctual," Nat said. "And it looks like you brought company."

Becky looked at Nat, not knowing what she should do. Part of her wanted to scream for help and announce that they were kidnapping her and were surely going to fit her for a Chicago overcoat. But something inside told her to just sit still, not say a word, and see what played out. Nat might have been part of this scheme all along.

"Oh yeah. Don't pay any attention to her. That's my brother's kid. She's in trouble. You know the kind."

Becky narrowed her eyes at Mrs. Gilmore. It was one thing to be called trouble. It was another thing completely to suggest she was *in trouble*.

"I don't care about your family business. I'm just looking for my samples. I can't promise my friend will be a regular buyer, but if he likes your stuff..." Nat said.

"He'll like it." Mrs. Gilmore waved her hand as if she'd heard enough. Becky watched as she reached down into the front seat and pulled up two big bottles. Hooch. Becky had seen enough of the illegal stuff that she was sure that was what it was. Heck, her father had a fella stop by monthly with the same kinds of bottles.

"I'll be in touch," Nat said without looking at Becky sideways.

Before she knew it, she watched Nat pull out of the field, clinging to the fella driving.

"Okay. Now that that's done, we can take care of the rest of our business," Mrs. Gilmore said.

With jerky, violent movements, she started her

car and drove roughly over the grass, grazing more than one car in the process. Becky gasped and looked down, terrified one of the bumps might cause Talbot to accidentally pull the trigger. She couldn't bear to sit there while he so carelessly held his gun on her.

"Slow down." Becky didn't even know the words had come out of her mouth until it was too late. "Or take that gun out of my side."

"What did you just say?" Talbot grumbled.

"Get that gun out of my side!" Becky hollered. "What are you, crazy? With these potholes? Are you trying to kill me?"

"That might eventually be the idea. It depends. What do you think you are worth to your father? He's not as dumb as he looks, is he?" Mrs. Gilmore chuckled from the front seat.

"What?" Becky hissed. "You said my father was an honorable man. You said he was a gentleman through and through."

"He is. That's why we are sure he'll pay a handsome sum to get his precious only child back. And that will be our ticket out of this town. My only regret is that I didn't take at least one of those old crows out at the pie tasting," Mrs. Gilmore cackled.

Becky stared at her silhouette as they drove. Mr.

Talbot jabbed Becky once more in the side, making her yelp and lose her temper.

"I said get that gun out of my side!" She elbowed him.

The gun went off and shot a hole clear through the front passenger seat. Becky's mouth hung open as Mrs. Gilmore slammed on the brakes, bringing the jalopy to a sudden halt and hurling all of them brutally forward. Mr. Talbot looked the most shocked; his mouth hung open, and his eyes bugged out.

"Look what you did to my seat!" she screamed at Becky.

For a second, Becky's Southern manners tried to kick in, and she was about to stutter out a long string of apologies. But Talbot no longer had his gun on her. Becky held her breath and dove out the open window, landing on the ground with a thud. As she scrambled to her feet, she knew she'd wrecked yet another pair of stockings. Her skirt was torn, and her blouse was covered in dirt. But adrenaline was coursing through her veins as she took off running back toward the fair. There had to be a car coming down this very road or maybe some people walking home.

It didn't take long for her to hear the thud-thud-

thud of Talbot's clodhoppers gaining on her. She was sure there was a set of lights ahead of her. Wildly, she waved her arms and screamed at the top of her lungs. However, Becky only got the word "help" out of her mouth twice before everything went black.

When she came to, a blurry image of the sign in front of Mrs. Gilmore's house was all she saw before she was hoisted over Talbot's shoulder and carried into the house. There would be no rubberneckers tonight. No busybodies watching who was coming and going. They'd all be at the last night of the fair, watching the fireworks. Becky regretted not sticking close to Stephen. Because of her stupidity, now she was seeing stars.

CHAPTER TWENTY-TWO

When Becky regained consciousness, she found herself in a stuffy, dark room at the bottom of some rickety wooden steps. A dim bulb glowed in the middle of the room but gave off no more light than a candle. When Becky blinked, the front of her head ached. When she turned to look behind her, the back of her head ached. When she reached up to touch the sore spots, she realized her hands were tied to the armrests of the chair she was sitting in.

At the memory of what had happened to put her in such a sorry state, Becky winced. She had been so close to getting away. But that sneaky devil, Mr. Talbot, had clunked her on the noggin. She was sure she'd have a goose egg from that on the back of her head and probably another on her forehead from when she had fallen flat on her face. Her dress was filthy.

As her head started to clear and she was able to focus, Becky noticed an old bathtub at the far end of the basement, along with several metal containers of what looked like turpentine. Next to them were enough sacks of potatoes to feed an army. She also saw huge washbasins stacked with corn, and Becky counted more than a dozen sacks of sugar. They were making their booze down here. The air was damp and perfect for fermenting the potatoes.

But it looked like they just let the stuff rot along the floor. Cobwebs shadowed a dirt floor littered with stacks of old, empty crates, half a dozen set mousetraps, and more than a dozen suitcases. Becky thought they were rather strange things to collect, especially since they were all ugly, worn-out bags that looked as if they had been dragged behind a train, left in the sun and rain, and kicked down a couple of hills for good measure.

Becky wondered how many times she had drunk Mrs. Gilmore's hooch without knowing it. And had she known there was a human skeleton next to all the ingredients, would she still have taken a snort?

A human skeleton?

Becky's mouth fell open. There, just a matter of a couple short feet away, a partially clothed skeleton was propped up in the corner, staring in Becky's direction with its empty eye sockets. She let out a wild yelp that caused a flurry of footsteps to come clomping down the rickety wooden staircase.

"Do you know how to shut your mouth?" Mrs. Gilmore barked.

"Where am I? And who is that?" Becky shouted, jerking her head in the skeleton's direction as she tugged on the ropes holding her wrists fast to the armrests.

"I told Talbot to stuff a rag in your mouth. But he said no. Said you could choke on it. He doesn't have a problem shooting you, but he won't let you choke. He's a real peach that way." Mrs. Gilmore huffed.

"Tell him I said thanks. Did he sh…shoot that person?" Becky stuttered.

"No. I killed that person. That was my husband. He was a lot like our friend," Mrs. Gilmore said.

"Who?"

"Why, Mr. Foxworthy, that's who. My husband also had a weakness for the ladies. And he was a real bruno when he drank. Sadly, he drank quite a bit of our inventory. I had to put an end to that. Not to mention Mr. Gilmore had a lot to say about my cooking. He said I couldn't even make a decent cup of joe."

Becky remembered forcing down Mrs. Gilmore's coffee the other day. In her opinion, the man hadn't been wrong.

"So you killed him?" Becky practically whispered the words.

"That's right. I slipped a little of that same rat poison into his oatmeal," Mrs. Gilmore said as she pointed to one of the many mousetraps along the floor. "And when it was done, Mr. Talbot helped me prop him up down here. He wasn't missed. No one came looking for him. I just told everyone he left with some woman. After all the years I gave to him. What was I going to do?" Mrs. Gilmore began to cry and sniffle, making Becky believe she was grief-stricken to this very day...until the creepy old woman started to laugh.

"You're crazy," Becky muttered. "And so is Mr. Talbot."

"Maybe so. But it made us a very pretty penny. I'll miss the old house. It has served me well. But there are a million old houses for an old lady like me to find her way into." Mrs. Gilmore smiled sweetly. "Why, if I showed up at the Mackenzie home and said I was an old aunt from a distant relative who died in the war and prattled on about losing my husband to pneumonia and having everything I own on my back, do you think someone like your mother wouldn't extend me every bit of Southern hospitality for as long a spell as I needed? There are a million Kitty Mackenzies out there," she said bitterly.

"You don't know my mother," Becky replied.

"I know she associates with Caroline Brower and Tilly Hindergast. I am leaving with a job only half-done, and that does cause me some distress. My hope was that I could have poisoned those two biddies at the same time I took out Foxworthy," Mrs. Gilmore said.

"What is wrong with you?" Becky shook her head.

"You see, he would have given me the blue ribbon. Of that I am certain. Then those old hens would have been so upset at the humiliating defeat that they would have had to taste my delicious blue ribbon–winning pie too. Their pride wouldn't have allowed for any other course of action." Mrs. Gilmore giggled and batted her lashes. "No one would suspect me. Harmless, abandoned old Mrs. Gilmore."

"My father will catch you. You might think that he's weak or stupid, but he'll find you, and you'll spend the rest of your life in the hoosegow. You and Mr. Talbot." Becky smirked.

"You know what? I think you need to put a sock in it," Mrs. Gilmore said and pulled a kerchief from her pocket. Her peaceful, old-lady face instantly transformed into the grimace of a hardened criminal. Becky tried to pull back, but Mrs. Gilmore was on her in two long strides. She didn't move like an infirm, helpless old lady. Becky bit down on her thumb when she tried to stuff the kerchief into her mouth.

"Oh, you brat! Why, I oughta…!" Mrs. Gilmore screamed before Mr. Talbot yelled down the stairs.

"Dummy up down there! We've got company!"

Becky wondered if the man ever spoke above a whisper.

Just then, there was a loud knock on the door. Mrs. Gilmore glared at Becky and pounced on her, shoving the kerchief into her mouth despite Becky's attempt to stop her.

Without another word, she turned and hurried up the stairs. There was muffled talking, and Becky heard someone outside yell for Mrs. Gilmore. It was Judge.

"Mrs. Gilmore. I need to talk to you. It's about my daughter!" Judge shouted.

Becky could hear the worry in his voice. They had been on such rocky terms lately that Becky had almost forgotten what his voice sounded like. But it was unmistakable. And if he walked into Mrs. Gilmore's house, it was all going to be over. She tried to spit out the kerchief, but it was no use.

Instead, she studied the ropes around her wrists. They were snug, but she was sure that if she tried, she could wiggle them loose. Her feet were not bound. They were the only parts of her body that she could move. Quickly, she looked around the basement. Becky's only hope was to break the chair and maybe get free that way. The brick foundation offered a hard wall for her to bang the chair into. But getting herself over there was going to be harder than it seemed.

Like a hunchback, Becky leaned forward. The wooden chair was thick and heavy as she lifted it awkwardly with her legs and back. If she fell, there would be a very good chance she'd be stuck, and the kerchief in her mouth would choke her to death long before her father would reach her.

With quick, precise steps, she inched her way closer and closer to the wall. Her idea was that if she could swing the chair against the brick a couple times, she might damage it enough to give herself some slack so she could wiggle out of the rope. It wasn't a great plan, but it was all she had.

With each strain of her legs and each painful step, Becky felt the sweat drip down her back. She was frantic to get to her father before Mrs. Gilmore did. What if she offered him some coffee and it wasn't just awful tasting? What if Mr. Talbot snuck up behind him and clunked him on the head?

Finally, she made it across the room. She sat in the chair for a moment to catch her breath. It was getting harder and harder to breathe with the kerchief in her mouth. She was trying to push it out with her tongue, but it was wedged in there too far.

Becky decided it was now or never. She got to her feet, still bent over, and swung her backside so far to the left that she reminded herself of Fanny's normal way of walking. With all her strength, she swiveled to the right and crashed the chair into the brick wall. It didn't break, but Becky heard a loud crack. One more might do it.

Upstairs, she could hear Mrs. Gilmore shouting. "Just a moment please! I'll be right there!"

She positioned herself again and swung the chair so far to the left that her back hurt. Then, with all her might, she brought it hard against the brick. This time, it did break. The ropes went loose around

Becky's wrists, and she was able to shake them off, letting everything clatter to the floor. She pulled the kerchief from her mouth.

If she ran up the stairs, Mrs. Gilmore and Mr. Talbot could catch her, and she'd be right back where she started. Her father might never know she was in the house. Or they might just do away with him right then and there. The heck with any ransom.

There was a small window just behind the remains of Mrs. Gilmore's husband. Becky ran to it. It took some doing, but she managed to stand on the sacks of potatoes next to the skeleton, only to sink into them. They were rotting and perfect for making booze but not so good as a step stool to escape. If only Mr. Gilmore wasn't in the way. But he was, and Becky only had one chance, maybe two, to get out of this dungeon. Her fingers just barely reached the window. There was no way she could pull herself up, and even if she could, she was ashamed to admit that her rump might not fit through the opening.

"Mr. Mackenzie," Becky heard Mrs. Gilmore say. "Please come in."

Becky's heart began to race. "No!" she screamed. She lost her balance and tumbled off the sacks of potatoes and nearly knocked over Mr. Gilmore.

Instead, she jerked backward and fell into the boxes of bottles used for the gin. It made an awful ruckus.

"That was just one of my tenants down in the basement," Mrs. Gilmore said.

Becky was about to dash up the stairs when she saw Mr. Talbot was already on his way down. She hadn't even heard him. The guy was as silent as dandelion spores catching on a silk spiderweb. He had his gun in his hand.

"Get out of my way, Mr. Talbot," Becky said.

He didn't say anything but kept coming down the steps. At the very bottom were a couple of set mousetraps. As he stepped from the last stair onto the dirt floor, his boot hit the trap, setting it off and making him jump. Becky reached down, grabbed a trap with a huge dead mouse in it, and tossed it at Mr. Talbot, making him lose his balance even more. As if he was trying to do the Charleston but couldn't master the steps, his arms went up as one foot flailed high while gravity pulled all of his weight to the ground. He let out a yelp, and his head pulled into his neck as he cringed and swatted away the loaded mousetrap.

As soon as his keister hit the floor, his gun went off.

"Daddy!" Becky shouted as she bolted up the stairs.

"What is that?" Becky heard Judge ask Mrs. Gilmore.

"Daddy!" she shouted again.

"Rebecca! Where is she? Tell me where she is, or I'll…"

Just as Judge was about to finish his threat, Becky burst through the basement door into the quaint, cute little kitchen in which she'd sipped bad coffee from Mrs. Gilmore.

"Daddy! She killed Mr. Foxworthy and her husband! He's downstairs!" Becky stammered as she rushed to her father.

"Becky!" He held her in his arms for only a brief second before scooting her behind him. "Don't you move, Mrs. Gilmore."

"Oh, I'm just an old woman. I don't know what you are talking about. Mr. Talbot…he's the one…he's the one who made me do it." Mrs. Gilmore suddenly shrank before Becky's eyes, turning from the grimacing, deadly bootlegger to a helpless spinster who couldn't lift a cat, let alone kill someone.

Just then, two coppers came barging in. "Are you all right, Judge? We got a tip you were here and that there was an incident of kidnapping," said one officer, whose jowls hung over the stiff collar of his uniform.

"She tried to take my daughter," Judge said, his voice cracking.

Becky looked up to see her father with tears in his eyes. "How did you ever know?" Becky asked. "How did you find me?"

"A flapper by the name of Nat Phine showed up at the house. She told me she was sure you were in some kind of trouble." Judge quickly wiped his eyes.

"Be careful, officers. Mr. Talbot is in the basement, and he has a gun. He's not a very good shot though," Becky said.

The officer with the jowls stayed with Mrs. Gilmore. The other went into the basement. Becky was afraid to leave them for fear that Mrs. Gilmore and Mr. Talbot might slip away. Especially that sneaky Mr. Talbot.

But after a just a few seconds, the officer came back up the stairs. His face was pale, and he shook his head. "Her accomplice is out cold. There's a nice distillery down there. But who is the skeleton?"

Both officers and Judge stared at Mrs. Gilmore, who chewed her dentures and said nothing.

Everything that had happened would be in the newspaper the next day. But Judge would manage to keep Becky's name out of it. He thought that would be for the best.

"If your mother finds out about it when she comes home, she'll…have kittens," Judge said as they drove back to the plantation.

"When is she coming back?" Becky asked, terrified but desperate to know.

"Tomorrow night," Judge said.

Becky let out a deep sigh.

CHAPTER TWENTY-THREE

The next day's newspapers reported that Mrs. Eleanor Gilmore and Rufus Talbot had been arrested in the poisoning of Mr. Foxworthy. They were also charged with bootlegging. But the real meat and potatoes of the story was the skeleton.

"It's so sad they refer to him as the skeleton," Becky said as she sipped her coffee the next morning.

"I can't believe that you were involved in it. Although I shouldn't be surprised. Wherever there is a seedy situation taking place, you seem to always be nearby," Fanny grumbled.

"What's the matter? Jealous?" Becky tittered.

"Hardly. I have to admit that until Stephen realized you were missing, we were having quite a time. We have a lot in common," Fanny said as she took a big bite of the biscuits and gravy piled high on her plate.

"That's what you were concerned with when I didn't show up?" Becky huffed.

It wasn't that she was surprised Fanny was focusing on herself. Just the fact that she was saying it so bluntly out loud and that she didn't mention Paris was what had Becky shocked.

"You aren't exactly known for your manners, Rebecca," Fanny said in between bites.

Unfortunately, Becky couldn't argue with Fanny there. She let out a deep breath and took a sip of coffee while she let those words sink in.

It was true. That was what had started this whole mess with her family. She'd had to sneak off to follow poor Vincent, who was doing nothing more than throwing away a bottle of giggle juice. And he had been doing that because of Judge. Becky wanted to ask her father about that, but he'd already left again.

Moxley had said he'd be back before ten, and Becky was going to clear the air with him then. It was going to be difficult, but she had to know why Bernice Foxworthy had been at their house at night and what was really going on with Kitty. She felt nervous even thinking about it. She was afraid that her father would tell her that things were bad, that Mama might not be coming home or that he might be leaving. What would she do if both her parents weren't there? Becky was ashamed to say that for a brief second, she wondered what the ladies in town would think. A divorce? The scandal!

After breakfast, she scooped up her sketchbook and pencils and went to the Old Brick Cemetery and spread out under her favorite tree, its hanging moss giving her plenty of shade.

Mr. Wilcox was walking past and gave her a wave hello, but today he didn't stop to chat. Instead, he faded away as he walked.

Becky sketched Mrs. Gilmore and Mr. Talbot. They were interesting subjects, as they were crinkly and deceptive. So much was in their eyes that Becky lost all track of time while she was drawing them. When Teeter came running up to the rusted front gate and stopped short, calling Becky's name, she nearly jumped out of her skin.

"What's the matter?" Becky asked with her hand to her chest.

"Mama said to tell you you've got a gentleman caller," Teeter said.

"Now, Teeter, when are you going to come in here and sit with me? It's a perfect place for a picnic with watermelon and some of your mama's cucumber sandwiches," Becky replied.

"I told you, Miss Becky. I don't want ghosts following me home," he said, looking around as if he might spot one any second.

"What if we had a picnic and I read you *Tarzan of the Jungle?*" Becky asked as she got to her feet and dusted off her dress.

"I don't know, Miss Becky." Teeter looked nervous.

"How about this. How about instead of reading in the cemetery, we read on the big porch swing?" Becky asked, giving Teeter an easy way out.

"Can we have a picnic on the porch?"

"I don't think it would be hardly worth it if we didn't," Becky said as she rubbed his head.

"Miss Becky, are you going to marry this man whose come calling?" Teeter asked.

"I don't know who it is," Becky replied matter-of-factly. "Can't say I'm going to marry a gent if I don't know who he is. That'd be crazy."

"He's big. And he brought lots of flowers with him," Teeter said.

"Well, what do you think? Should I marry him?" Becky asked.

"No. Not yet. I don't want you to get married until I'm grown," Teeter said.

"Why not?" Becky could hardly wait to hear his answer.

"So I can make sure the fellow is good enough. When I'm big, if I have to throw him off the land, I'll be able to do it," Teeter replied confidently.

"I think that's a splendid idea. You go on inside and see if your mama needs any help," Becky said as they came within view of the house.

Becky hadn't given Adam a second thought since she'd gotten home the night before. But there he was, dressed fine with his hair combed and, as Teeter had said, a lot of flowers. She regretted that Teeter wasn't grown at this present moment and couldn't toss him off their land.

"Yes, Miss Becky," Teeter said before taking off at breakneck speed for the back of the house.

"Hi, Beck," Adam said.

Becky hated that he looked so sharp.

He smiled, but the weight of his actions pulled his lips down quickly when Becky didn't return the smile.

"What are you doing here?"

"Becky, I can't tell you how sorry I am. I made a mistake, and I swear, I can't imagine planning a future that doesn't have you in it," Adam said.

He continued to tell her about the first time he saw her and the way she always made him feel and that he'd never before felt the kind of pain he felt now knowing he'd hurt her.

"I appreciate that, Adam. I have to go now. I've got things to do today," Becky lied. She had nothing to do. Her mother wasn't around, her father wasn't back yet, Lucretia was busy, and Moxley was out playing. The only person inside was Fanny.

"No, you don't." Adam stepped closer. "Come on. Can't we take a drive out into the country? Maybe share a Coca-Cola at that little diner off the beaten path where we went before?"

Adam's blue eyes were almost hypnotic. There was nothing stopping Becky from going with him. If she did, she'd have to accept what he'd done and get over it quickly. She thought about what Teddy and Martha might think. Would they be upset with her if she so easily forgave Adam? Would they be upset with her if she didn't forgive him?

"I'm sorry," Becky said, "but it will take a little more than flowers to fix this. I never stepped out on you, Adam. I never drank so much or danced so close with a fella that it could ever even be possible."

"It was just one time. And it was just necking. It won't ever happen again," Adam pleaded.

His eyes became red, and for a moment Becky thought maybe she was being too hard on him. But before she could say the words "okay" and "I forgive you," she opened her mouth, and a whole different sentence came out.

"If a man steps out once, he'll do it again." Becky had heard that saying a million times at the hen coop while getting her hair done or at the department store waiting for her mother or Fanny in the fitting rooms.

"Becky, please. Don't do this," Adam pleaded.

"I wasn't the one who did it," she said before walking past Adam and up the porch steps.

Just then, the sound of a car coming up the long drive could be heard. Becky let out a sigh of relief. It was her father.

Judge parked his car behind Adam's jalopy. The look on his face was crystal clear, as he knew what Adam had done. If Adam had thought Becky was going to be a hard nut to crack, he had no idea that appeasing her father would be like trying to cut diamond.

"Hello, Mr. Mackenzie," Adam said nervously.

"Have you completed your business here, son?" Judge asked softly.

"I guess…well, kind of," Adam stuttered.

"Then I guess it's best you be on your way." He stood toe-to-toe with Adam, and Becky was shocked to see her father looking so angry. Adam shrank down, nodded, and put out his hand to Judge. Becky watched her father shake Adam's hand casually then give him the bum's rush as if he was an unwanted encyclopedia salesman.

She went inside the house only to find Fanny hurrying up the stairs. She'd been watching and hadn't had enough time to go hang on Adam like Becky was sure she wanted to. Of course, it wasn't any big deal for Fanny now, not when Stephen was paying attention to her redheaded cousin.

Becky loitered in the foyer until her father came in. Becky heard Adam's jalopy crank up and grow quieter and quieter as he drove away.

As soon as Judge stepped inside the door, he smiled at Becky.

"You knew what he did?" Becky asked.

"Vincent told me before he…" Judge said. "He said he thought I should know."

Becky nodded.

"Are you all right?" he asked her.

"Just ducky." Becky smiled and shrugged before the tears flooded her eyes.

She'd been holding it in so long, waiting to talk to Kitty, waiting to lay her head in her mother's lap while she stroked her hair, but she just couldn't wait anymore. When Judge opened his arms to her, she rushed to him and cried into his shirt like a little girl.

"It'll be all right, Becky. You'll get through this. If you survived Eleanor Gilmore, you can survive a chump like Adam White," Judge said, making Becky chuckle. He pulled a white handkerchief from his pocket and handed it to her.

"Daddy, why was Beatrice Foxworthy here the other night?" Becky sniffed before she pulled back and looked up at her father.

"You saw her?"

"I was on the trellis," Becky replied.

"You were going to find out sooner or later. Beatrice Foxworthy and I have known each other since we were children in school. Your mother doesn't like her much," Judge said.

Becky braced herself to hear the worst. Here it was, coming at her at full speed. She took a step back from her father and looked at his face. He didn't look pitiful and awkward like Adam just had. In fact,

Judge looked proud and confident. Becky thought that made it worse.

"Clem Foxworthy had spent a good deal of her money. Beatrice knew she was going to be in financial trouble if she didn't make that money up somehow. She'd thought she had more time. But now that he was gone, she was left with his debts. Debts she had no idea about. Debts that made Vincent No-cent look like a financial genius."

"Oh, that's terrible," Becky said, not really understanding what any of this had to do with her family.

"Beatrice had asked for my help months ago because of our history together. And because she knew that I wouldn't say a word about it to anyone," Judge said. He gave Becky a look that suggested he was trusting her with the same assumption.

"Not even Mama?" Becky asked.

"Not even Mama," Judge said. "At least not yet. I'd never kept a secret from your mother. I love her more now than I did the day we exchanged vows. I just needed some time to get things in order before I told her."

"Told her what?" Becky asked.

"Told her that I just bought four hundred more acres of land. I've been tending to it for the past several weeks. It was a bit of land that was neglected and overrun but that had been Beatrice's for some time. I don't know all the details. Someone died and left it to her, but she's no farmer, and we all know Clem wasn't good with too much." Judge shrugged.

"But you were so angry with her, and you both were fighting and…"

"Becky, I'd made a promise to Beatrice that I wouldn't say anything to anyone until the deal was done. That way no one would know about Beatrice's financial troubles. We made a business deal, and that's that. I just needed your mother to trust me. No one expected Clem to suddenly be dead. I had to do more work in these last few days before the creditors started asking questions. I wanted to tell Kitty, but I was on tenterhooks," he said, shaking his head. And smirking. "It's that red hair. The temper."

"So that's where you've been rushing off to?" Becky asked, wiping her nose with the white kerchief he'd given her.

"That's where I've been," Judge admitted. "So dry your eyes and grab your clutch."

"Why?" Becky smiled.

"I'm going to show you our new plot of land," Judge said. "What would you think if we started growing corn?"

"I think that sounds swell," Becky replied.

As much as she was heartbroken over Adam, she couldn't help but be excited by this news. As they drove together, Becky felt like she was enjoying the sun on her face after a long row of rainy days. Judge sang some corny old tune that only he knew the words to and whistled as they made their way down some quiet dirt roads to their final destination. When they pulled up to the wooden gate that led to the property, Becky read the sign posted there and gasped out loud.

"Kathleen Hill! Oh, Daddy, that's beautiful!" Becky squealed.

"Do you think when your mama sees it, she'll forgive me?" Judge asked, smiling with pride at his new purchase.

"Well, you might have to do a little begging. But I think eventually she will. You might want to buy her some flowers and candy. You know how much she loves sweets," Becky added.

They got out of the car and walked hand in hand like they had done so many times when she was a little girl. They talked about the land, and Judge explained how he had run into Vincent No-cent, nearly slicing him into bits when he discovered him sleeping in the weeds.

Becky looked up at her father as he spoke. His

voice was quiet and gentle as he talked about Vincent and how sad he was that he'd been killed.

"He could have left with Lucille. But he dropped one vice and picked up another. They will always be your undoing," Judge mused.

"Be happy with what you have, right, Daddy?" Becky said as she squeezed his hand.

"That's right, Becky." He squeezed back.

CHAPTER TWENTY-FOUR

"*I* can't believe we are going to this woman's house again," Fanny griped.

"Fanny, if you complain one more time, I'm going to sock you right in the chops," Becky snapped as they walked up the dirt drive of the old colonial in which Nat Phine lived.

"I hope she's got some hooch. I'm parched," Martha said as she patted her hair into place and smoothed out her dress.

"I'm sure she will. That's what she was buying from Mrs. Gilmore," Becky replied.

"Can you believe you were in that old biddy's house, and in her basement was her dead husband? And you said you had a cup of coffee. She could have slipped you a mickey that put you six feet under."

Martha gasped. "Oh, Becky, sometimes I know how your mother feels. You can be crazy at times."

"I didn't know she was a button man. Who would have thought that old lady was a professional killer?" Becky replied, shrugging.

As they neared the front door, they heard music coming out the open windows.

"I do hope she isn't entertaining," Fanny said with a frown.

Just then, the front door opened, and one of the finest examples of Uncle Sam's sailors filled the frame. He had broad shoulders and black hair cut short on the sides and slicked back on top. He sported a starched white uniform that was wide around his ankles and had a black tie around the collar.

"You must be Becky." He smiled right at her.

"I am. Don't tell me we're being invaded," Becky shot back smartly.

"Ha. I heard all about you from my sister. She had a feeling you'd be coming to see her sometime soon." He stepped aside and held the door open for them. "I'm James Phine, Natalie's baby brother. But you can call me Jimmy."

"Well, James Phine, I'm here to see your sister. Is she at home?" Becky asked, looking at him squarely while trying desperately not to trip over herself. He was as easy on the eyes as a plate of watermelon on a hot July afternoon.

"She is. She's in the kitchen," James said, hanging on the door a little as he watched Becky walk in.

Two more gents wearing the same uniform popped up from the parlor, where they had been gathered around the Victrola. They nearly tripped each other to get introduced to Fanny and Martha. But once James shut the door, he followed Becky into the kitchen.

"I was hoping you'd come and see me!" Nat called from her stove. "Are you doing all right? I knew that old biddy was trouble, but my friend, Mr. Jones, was hoping to branch out to a couple of new buyers."

"Oh, Nat," Becky gushed and went up to the robust woman, who was wearing an expensive blue dress with brown trim. Her fingers still glistened with big rings and red nail polish. Her red hair was tucked into an elegant turban. Becky hugged her tightly.

"Honey, now come on. You didn't think when I saw you there that I was going to let that old liar abscond with you. You're good stock. I don't give up on good stock." Nat winked.

"What happened?" James asked as he shuffled into the kitchen.

"You met my brother, Jimmy," Nat said as she stirred something that smelled wonderfully minty.

"I did." Becky smiled.

"Nat, can you step away from that concoction for a second?" Jimmy asked.

"What for?" Nat snapped.

"I need you in the other room," Jimmy said from behind Becky. When she turned around, he smiled at her, making her roll her eyes but blush nonetheless.

"Fine. Rebecca, honey, will you stir this sugar and bourbon so we can all enjoy some mint juleps?" Nat asked as she handed the wooden spoon to Becky.

"Mint juleps? Of course I can," Becky said as she took over in front of the stove.

She looked around the kitchen, which was plain but elegant. The curtains hanging across the window over the sink were clean and white. The rectangular table in the center of the kitchen had enough chairs for five people. Becky imagined Nat entertaining strange characters of all sorts of experiences and backgrounds. She thought she'd love to introduce Madame Cecelia to her. What a grand time they'd have.

"You are staying for mint juleps, aren't you?" Nat

asked as she sashayed back into the kitchen.

"Oh, wild horses couldn't drag me away. What was that all about, if you don't mind my asking?" Becky jerked her thumb toward the door through which Nat and her brother had disappeared for a moment.

"My little brother wanted to know if you were available," Nat said quietly. "I didn't see a ring on your finger, and I didn't think someone who gets herself into wild situations like you just did had any ball and chain waiting for her. I hope I guessed right."

Becky smirked. "You did. But your brother is in the Navy. Won't he be leaving soon?"

"He's stationed at Fort Benning for the time being. Unfortunately for me, that means he'll be here more than he'll be on base." Nat chuckled. "I love him, but he eats like a country mule."

"Oh, I see," Becky said.

She knew she'd just gotten off the ropes with Adam. Her heart would need time to heal. Without hesitation, she explained that to Nat. There was something about her that made Becky feel she'd understand.

"Honey, what you need is to have a little fun. Look, I'm not hoping for wedding bells. I just know

Jimmy. And from what I can tell with you, I think you might have a little in common. Get to know him." Nat winked.

"I didn't expect all this," said Becky. "I was just stopping by to tell you thank you for, well, literally saving my skin. How did you get to my father so quickly?"

"Well, let's just say my escort for the evening has a few connections with Savannah's finest. It just took mentioning your name, and they all knew who you were and who your father was. I got your address quick and hightailed it right over there. I told him not to worry, and that we'd get the police to meet him. But I noticed there wasn't any mention of you or your father in the papers."

"No, my father pulled a few strings to keep me out of it." Becky smiled.

"That's smart. If you're going to get your name in the papers, be sure it's for something worthwhile. Escaping the clutches of a bootlegging face stretcher and her clunky old accomplice might not be the notoriety you want," Nat said, making Becky laugh.

"When you put it that way..." Becky accepted the silver cup filled with ice and a few sprigs of mint leaves.

"Now, how about some lively conversation?" Nat

asked. "That dame hung up on Paris, is she here too?"

"Cousin Fanny. Yes." Becky sighed and rolled her eyes.

"Great. Max has been to Paris. They are perfect for each other. Sorry if your friend Martha is looking for an arm to hang on; Jasper has a girl back home." Nat shrugged as she poured the concoction into a huge, ice-filled glass pitcher and placed it on a big silver platter with enough cups for everyone. "Beck, would you grab that bucket of ice?"

"Of course. And that's okay. Martha and my dear friend Teddy are practically handcuffed," Becky replied happily.

She didn't really want to talk to Jimmy. She wanted to hear about Nat and the things she'd done that had gotten her to this stage in life. She had beautiful pictures and so many books and elegant furniture yet she was anything but stuffy or snooty.

"All right, kids. Here's a little something to wet your whistles," Nat said as she brought in the tray.

Just then, there was another knock on the door. Without waiting for Nat to answer, a couple who looked as exotic and interesting as she did came in. They were introduced as Mr. and Mrs. Wooloo, just back from Australia.

Becky listened to them as they gushed about their trip and the things they had seen. She listened to Nat, who asked for the differences between Australia and New Zealand since she'd only been to the latter.

"Can you believe all the places Nat has been?" Jimmy asked as he sat down next to Becky.

"It's amazing. You know, I have a friend who is, well, she's a Gypsy, and she reads fortunes and has a wonderful little shop in the middle of the city. I think Nat would adore her," Becky spilled. "I know some people think Gypsies are not on the up-and-up. But Cecelia is. Her mother Ophelia, though— she's a bit scary."

"When I was in Italy, there was an old woman there who wore a black dress, her hair pulled back in a bun so tight it looked painful. She would read your future in chicken giblets," Jimmy said, making Becky gasp and laugh.

"You were in Italy?"

"I've been to a few interesting places," Jimmy said.

"Wow. I'd love to travel someday. I bet Savannah seems kind of sleepy compared to all that." Becky smiled and took a sip of her julep.

"Not anymore," Jimmy replied.

ABOUT THE AUTHOR

Harper Lin is a *USA TODAY* bestselling cozy mystery author.

When she's not reading or writing, she loves hiking, doing yoga, and hanging out with her family and friends.

For a complete list of her books by series, visit her website.

www.HarperLin.com